NOOSE FOR A LADY

Sent to trial for the murder, by poison, of her husband John, Margaret Hallam is convicted and sentenced to death. Her appeal is dismissed and the Home Secretary refuses a reprieve. Simon Gale, an old friend of Margaret, returns from painting in Italy and learns about her case. Whilst refusing to believe she's guilty, the only way he can save her is to discover the real murderer's identity. But there are no concrete clues and time is against him . . .

GERALD VERNER

NOOSE FOR A LADY

Complete and Unabridged

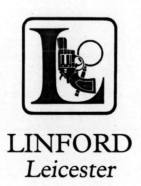

LINFORD
Leicester

First published in Great Britain

First Linford Edition
published 2013

A catalogue record for this book is available
from the British Library.

ISBN 978–1–4448–1547–4

Published by
F. A. Thorpe (Publishing)
Anstey, Leicestershire

Set by Words & Graphics Ltd.
Anstey, Leicestershire
Printed and bound in Great Britain by
T. J. International Ltd., Padstow, Cornwall

This book is printed on acid-free paper

1

I

From a window high up in the court a dusty shaft of sunlight slanted down and touched the woman in the dock. It rested, palely and without heat, across her shoulders, illuminating one side of her face, and leaving the other side in shadow. She stared straight in front of her, expressionless and without emotion, as the Clerk of Arraigns addressed the jury.

'Members of the jury, are you agreed upon your verdict?'

The Foreman, a small, dapper man, who looked as though he might be in the Civil Service, said, nervously:

'We are.'

'Do you find the accused, Margaret Elizabeth Hallam, guilty or not guilty of murder?'

'Guilty.'

A whispering rustle swept through the

court, like a wind in the hush before a storm.

'You say,' said the Clerk of Arraigns, unemotionally, 'that she is guilty, and is that the verdict of you all?'

'It is,' said the Foreman with dry lips, his eyes averted from the woman in the dock.

'Margaret Elizabeth Hallam,' said the Clerk of Arraigns, 'you have pleaded not guilty to murder, and put yourself upon your country. That country has now found you guilty. Have you anything to say why sentence should not be pronounced upon you according to the law?'

'I can only repeat that I am not guilty.' The voice was steady and low but very clear.

'Is that all you have to say?' asked the Judge.

'What else can I say?' she answered. 'It's the truth. I didn't do it . . . '

The Judge's Clerk draped the square of black silk over the judge's wig. The chaplain stood up.

'Margaret Elizabeth Hallam,' said the Judge in a dry, brittle voice that was not loud but reached to every corner of the crowded court. 'The jury have found you guilty of the murder, by poison, of your husband, John Hallam. With that verdict I entirely concur. Upon the evidence which has been placed before this court, no other verdict would be possible. There only remains for me to pass upon you the sentence prescribed by the law.' The brittle voice paused and then went on: 'Which is: that you be taken from this place to a lawful prison, and thence to a place of execution, and that you there be hanged by the neck until you are dead; and that your body be afterwards buried within the precincts of the prison in which you have been confined after your conviction, and may the Lord have mercy on your soul.'

'Amen,' murmured the chaplain.

The woman in the dock stood rigidly, staring in front of her, the shaft of sunlight now full upon her. She remained thus, as though turned to stone, until one of the wardresses touched her gently on the shoulder . . .

Old Joshua Mayhew, of Hicks, Thornley & Mayhew, peered shortsightedly across his desk at the girl who was sitting in the shabby leather chair facing him.

'I am — er — very much afraid, Miss Hallam,' he said, shaking his head like a venerable tortoise, 'there is nothing more we can do. Your stepmother's appeal has been dismissed, as you know. It is unfortunate, but there were no legal grounds upon which it could be upheld.' He coughed, two quick, dry little coughs. 'The Home Secretary, I regret to say, has — er — signified his unwillingness to move in the matter of a reprieve . . . '

'But surely, Mr. Mayhew,' interrupted Jill Hallam, 'there is still *something* we can do? I'm quite sure my stepmother isn't guilty . . . '

The old lawyer took off his glasses and blinked several times. This was really very difficult — very difficult indeed.

'Unfortunately,' he said, 'the evidence is all the other way. I sympathize with you very deeply. As your late father's legal adviser for many years, you will realize that the matter is extremely painful to me. But there is nothing I can do. It would be wrong of me to hold out hope where there is none . . . '

'Can't you think of anything?' she demanded.

He moved his head slowly but firmly from side to side.

'I'm afraid not,' he said.

Jill Hallam frowned. She looked, he thought, very young and childish with her fair hair and blue eyes — very like her mother too . . . The mouth was firm, though, and the chin obstinate . . .

'Do you mean,' she said, 'that we've just got to sit still and let Margaret suffer for something she didn't do?'

Mayhew coughed. It was a habit when he was uncomfortable or embarrassed.

'Are you *sure* that that will be the case?' he asked.

'Of course,' she answered quietly. 'If I weren't I shouldn't be worrying . . . Oh, can't you understand? I've lived with Margaret — in the same house — for over three years . . . You can't do that and not know what a person's like — *really* like . . . '

'Miss Hallam,' he put in quietly, 'it's sometimes very difficult to — er — realize that a person we are fond of, particularly a close relation, should be capable of a terrible act like — er — murder. A great number of people have had, however, to face up to the fact . . . '

'You're quite convinced that she's guilty, aren't you?' she said.

'Yes, candidly, I am,' he admitted.

'Oh, I wish I could make you see . . . ' She beat her knee impatiently with a gloved hand.

'I followed the trial very closely,' he said, 'and there was no other conclusion to be drawn from the evidence . . . '

'But . . . '

'Your father died from an overdose of barbitone,' he went on, 'administered in a glass of hot — er — whisky and milk. This mixture was prepared by Mrs. Hallam herself, and taken by her to your father in his study the last thing before she retired for the night. Nobody could have had access to this whisky and milk except your father and Mrs. Hallam . . . '

'I know all this, Mr. Mayhew,' said Jill impatiently. 'What's the use . . . '

He held up a thin hand.

'Please allow me to finish,' he said. 'The only fingerprints found on the glass were those of your father and Mrs. Hallam. In the remains of the whisky and milk, sufficient barbitone was found to show that the original contents must have contained a lethal dose. For some time past, Mrs. Hallam had been taking a preparation of barbitone for insomnia. She kept her supply of the drug in a locked drawer in her bedroom, the key to which she carried in her handbag. Two days before your father's death, Mrs. Hallam purchased, on a prescription from her doctor, a fresh bottle of barbitone containing twenty-five five-grain tablets. When this bottle was found in her drawer there were only *three* tablets in it. She could not have used twenty-two tablets in two days, and she was unable to say what had become of them . . . '

'Why are you going over all this again?'

'Because I want to show you how very

unlikely it is that any mistake has been made . . . '

'Oh, I know it all *sounds* as though she must have done it,' said Jill, 'but I'm sure there is a mistake, all the same . . . '

'And I am equally sure that you are wrong,' he answered. 'The case for the prosecution was very strong — very strong indeed. The defence had no reasonable answer to it. The motive . . . '

'That was ridiculous,' she declared. 'Father and Margaret were always rowing over something or other . . . '

'But this particular row was different,' said Mr. Mayhew. 'On this occasion your father threatened to alter his will. Had he done so it might have made a very considerable difference to Mrs. Hallam's financial expectations . . . '

'Father threatened all sorts of things when he was in a temper,' she said. 'He didn't always mean them . . . '

'Possibly,' agreed Mr. Mayhew. 'In this instance, however, there is evidence that he did mean to carry out his threat . . . '

'You mean the appointment he made over the telephone with you?'

'Exactly.'

'But he didn't say anything about his will . . . '

'Not specifically . . . '

'Then he might have wanted to see you about anything . . . '

'Your father was overheard by the — er — housekeeper, Mrs. Barrett, to declare his intention of altering his will. Almost immediately afterwards he rang me up to make an appointment. I think we may safely assume that it was for that purpose.'

'You're not being very helpful, are you?' said Jill with a sigh.

'I'm very, very sorry,' said the old lawyer, 'but you must see, my dear, there is nothing I can do. The only advice I can offer you is to accept the situation . . . '

'I'm not going to,' she said strenuously. 'I can't . . . '

'Miss Hallam, be sensible. Everything possible has already been done . . . '

'No, it hasn't,' she retorted, 'There's still something that hasn't been done, and that's to find out the truth. Margaret didn't poison my father — I'm sure she didn't. There's been a mistake — a horrible mistake somewhere, and I'm going to try and find out where . . . '

He shook his head helplessly.

'You won't do any good . . . '

'I can try,' she declared. 'I can try to find out what *really* happened that night at Easton Knoll, and, if I can't get anyone to help me, I'll do it by myself . . . '

III

Superintendent Shelford looked at the filled-in form which the constable had put on his desk.

'Jill Hallam?' he muttered, frowning. 'What does she want to see me for?'

'It's on the form, sir,' said the constable, helpfully.

'H'm . . . yes . . . Where is she — in the waiting room?'

'Yes, sir.'

'All right, show her up,' said Shelford. He leaned back in his chair and rubbed his eyes. He was still gently stroking his forehead when Jill was shown in.

'Come in, Miss Hallam,' he said. 'Sit down, will you?'

She sat on the chair he indicated.

'You want to see me in connection with your stepmother, Mrs. Hallam, I believe,' he said.

She nodded.

'You were in charge of the investigation into my father's death, weren't you?' she asked.

'That's right, Miss Hallam,' he replied. 'I don't exactly see . . . '

'Are you quite satisfied that my stepmother is guilty?' she asked.

'Yes, I've no doubt at all,' he answered. 'Everything pointed to her from the start, and every fresh fact we came across confirmed our original view. It was a perfectly straightforward case . . . '

'I was hoping to persuade you to make further inquiries . . . ' she began.

'Can't be done, I'm afraid, Miss Hallam,' he said.

'But — supposing there's been a mistake . . . '

'There hasn't,' broke in Shelford. 'Don't you run away with any false notion

11

like that, Miss Hallam. We don't make mistakes at the Yard — not in a murder case, you know. We make pretty certain we've got the right person before we take any action.'

'You *could* be wrong, though, couldn't you?' she said. 'In this instance?'

She leaned forward, resting her hand on the desk. 'Think how dreadful it would be if you were . . . '

'Now listen, Miss Hallam,' said Shelford. 'The whole thing is over and done with. We put our case before the court, and Mrs. Hallam was found guilty. It's nothing more to do with us. We're out of it. If you had any fresh evidence — *real* evidence — to offer us — well, that'd be a different matter. Naturally we should have to take notice of that, but . . . '

'But you're not disposed to find fresh evidence yourself?' she said.

'I don't think it exists,' he answered bluntly. 'You see, if Mrs. Hallam didn't put that poison in the whisky and milk, someone else must have . . . '

'That's obvious,' she said.

'Exactly — and there just wasn't

anybody else. We went into all that thoroughly at the time. She had the opportunity, the means and the motive — she was the only person who had. The defence tried to make out that it was suicide, but there was nothing to back it up . . . You're not suggesting that, are you?'

'No, because I don't believe it for a moment,' she answered. 'My father wouldn't have done that — he always hated the thought of death . . . '

'There you are, you see? So we come back to Mrs. Hallam . . . '

'Or to — *somebody*,' she said.

He looked at her quickly.

'You don't happen to have any particular person in mind, do you?' he asked.

She shook her head.

'No . . . no, of course not,' she said.

'And you can take it from me there isn't anyone, Miss Hallam. If you'll forgive me for saying so you're letting sentiment blind you to the facts . . . '

'I suppose that's how it looks to you . . . '

'There's no other way of looking at it,' he said. 'If I were you, I wouldn't think any more about it. You'll only be wasting your time. It's no good flogging a dead horse . . .'

'I did hope,' she said, 'that something could be done . . .'

'Try and convince yourself that she did do it,' he advised. 'She did, you know — there's no doubt of it. You won't find it so bad then . . .'

Rather wearily she rose to her feet. There was no further use in prolonging the interview.

'I suppose I might as well go,' she said. 'It was very good of you to see me, Superintendent. I'm sorry to have wasted your time.'

IV

Margaret Hallam looked up as the key turned in the lock of the cell door.

'There's a visitor for you, Hallam,' said the wardress curtly.

'For me . . . ?'

'Yes, come along . . . '

Margaret hesitated, glanced at the stolid figures of the two wardresses who kept watch over her day and night, working in eight hour shifts, so that she was never left alone, and then followed the third along the stone corridor. Their footsteps echoed with a hollow unreal ring. At a door at the end, the wardress paused.

'In here,' she said, and ushered Margaret into the visitors' room.

It was a bare apartment with a wide bench running down the centre.

Jill looked round as her stepmother came in.

'Hello, Margaret,' she said.

'Hello, Jill,' said Margaret.

Almost unconsciously they moved towards each other, but the voice of the wardress stopped them.

'Keep on either side of the table, please.'

'Oh, I'm sorry — I always forget,' Jill stopped abruptly. 'It seems so silly . . . '

'It's regulations, miss,' said the woman.

'But I can't see why,' said Jill. 'What

15

harm would it do if . . . '

'Visitors must keep the regulation distance from the prisoner, miss,' said the wardress.

'They're afraid you might slip me something, Jill,' said Margaret.

'Slip you . . . ?' Jill looked puzzled.

'They take great care to see that — nothing can happen to you — prematurely,' said Margaret bitterly.

'Oh — I see what you mean . . . '

'That's why they're always watching you — day and night — just in case,' said Margaret. 'They never leave you alone for a second. That's the worst part of it — almost — never having any privacy . . . '

'Yes, I should hate that,' said Jill.

'It's beastly. I suppose you could get used to it in time — but they don't give you time. Did you see Mayhew?'

'Yes, I saw him . . . I'm afraid it wasn't much good . . . '

'I didn't think it would be,' said Margaret quietly. 'He never liked me, you know. He did his best to stop John marrying me — I wish to Heaven he'd succeeded . . . Well, there doesn't seem to be much we can do now, does there?'

'Mayhew can't do anything, but I haven't given up yet,' said Jill.

'What can you do, Jill, on your own?' said Margaret. 'There's so little time — seven days, that's all — just seven days . . . '

'It's not hopeless,' Jill tried to infuse into her voice a confidence that she didn't feel. 'If I only had some idea where to start . . . '

'I can't help you,' Margaret shook her head helplessly. 'I've gone all over it again and again. I lie awake at night thinking and thinking — remembering every little detail and trying to find something that's been overlooked — and there's nothing . . . nothing . . . '

'There must be, Margaret,' said Jill, 'if we only knew where to look for it. Oh, I wish I'd been there that night — at Easton Knoll. I might have seen or heard something . . . '

'Perhaps if you'd been there it wouldn't have happened — I don't know — I don't know, Jill. Even if you had been at home you'd probably have been in bed and asleep. It was late when I took John his whisky and milk — nearly midnight . . . '

'What was he doing when you left him?'

'Reading — one of those beastly books of his . . . '

'Father was a queer man in some ways,' said Jill.

'He was very — cruel,' said Margaret. 'He enjoyed seeing people suffer — not physically but mentally.' Her mouth twisted into a little smile that had no mirth in it. 'He'd have loved this — it's just the kind of situation he'd have revelled in . . . I wonder, sometimes, whether he didn't plan it all . . . '

'Oh, no, Margaret,' Jill protested, 'he couldn't . . . '

'No, he'd never have done anything to hurt *himself*,' answered her stepmother, 'not even for the pleasure of hurting someone else. There'd have been no fun if he couldn't watch . . . '

Jill looked at Margaret anxiously. She had never understood why this woman, attractive and very little older than

18

herself, had come to marry her father in the first place. She said, in a low voice:

'You must have hated him . . . '

'No, I didn't hate him,' said Margaret. 'I was sorry for him — in a way . . . '

'Somebody hated him,' said Jill.

'Yes — I suppose so . . . unless it was an accident . . . '

'It couldn't have been. That stuff must have been put in the whisky and milk deliberately . . . '

'But who could have done it. There was nobody in the house but ourselves and the servants — and they'd all gone to bed . . . '

'The servants could have had no reason . . . ' A sudden idea seemed to occur to Jill and she put it eagerly into words. 'Listen, Margaret — supposing somebody called to see father — after you left him — you wouldn't have known, would you?'

'No . . . I don't think so,' replied Margaret. 'I was very tired — I fell asleep almost at once . . . '

'Somebody *could* have come — very late.' A tinge of excitement crept into Jill's voice. 'They *could*, couldn't they?'

'It's no good, Jill,' said Margaret. 'The police went into all that . . . '

'I know, but don't you see? It's the *only* explanation. Somebody must have come — they *must* . . . '

'But who? Who would be likely . . . ?'

'I don't know,' Jill clung desperately to the idea, 'at least it's something to work on, isn't it?'

Some of her enthusiasm coummunicated itself to the elder woman.

'If — if it *could* be proved — *proved* — that somebody *did* come — it would make a difference, wouldn't it?'

'Of course it would — *all* the difference, Margaret. There would *have* to be a fresh inquiry then.'

'Nobody was seen — they couldn't have been — or the police would have known about it . . . '

'They might not — there wouldn't have been any witnesses . . . '

'Then how can you possibly *prove* anything?'

'I can try,' said Jill.

'Oh, Jill, if you could — if only you could . . . '

'I've got to — it's the only way . . . '

'You'll have to be quick,' whispered Margaret, 'very quick. There isn't much time left . . . '

2

I

Jill left the prison and took a bus to Piccadilly Circus. There was some time before her train left to take her back to the country and the restful comforts of Easton Knoll, the lovely old house in which she had spent the greater part of her life, and she decided that what she wanted just at that moment, wanted more than anything else, was tea. There was a restaurant opposite the place were the bus stopped and she went in. The place was very crowded but she managed to find a table and sat down with a sigh of relief.

After a long delay a waitress condescended to take notice of her presence.

'Only a pot o' tea, miss?' said the girl, when Jill gave her order. 'No cakes or anything?'

'No, thank you — just tea, please.'

The waitress sniffed and went away. Jill

lit a cigarette and looked around her. There was some kind of altercation going on near the entrance but a pillar obscured her view, and she couldn't see what it was about. Presently a deep, booming voice reached her ears. 'No room?' it roared, rising above the chatter and clatter of the place. 'Nonsense, my good girl. There is an empty chair at that table over there — where that lady is sitting. I can think of no valid reason why *I* should not occupy it. May I suggest that at the first opportunity you consult an oculist? Warne, of Wimpole Street is an excellent man.'

With an apologetic and flustered manageress twittering in his wake, a huge man in a rumpled suit of Harris tweed came striding over towards Jill's table.

'Madam,' he cried, when he was still several yards away, in a voice that effectually drowned all other sounds, 'I am sure you can have no objection if we share this table? Should your imagination suggest a motive other than a lack of accommodation elsewhere, I can assure you, that it requires a considerable amount of spring cleaning . . . '

'Please sit down, Mr. Gale,' said Jill.

The big man's shaggy eyebrows shot upwards and he tugged at a belligerent beard.

'Eh?' he shouted, 'Eh? I'm afraid I don't . . .'

'You *are* Simon Gale, aren't you?' said Jill.

'I am,' he agreed, 'but . . .'

'Then sit down and don't make so much fuss,' she said. 'Everybody's looking at you.'

He snapped his fingers contemptuously, but he sat down.

'Who are you?' he demanded.

'I'm Jill Hallam. Don't you remember? Margaret introduced us. It was rather a long time ago . . .'

'Ah!' exclaimed the bearded man. 'I've got it now. You're Maggie's stepdaughter . . . Here, waitress!' He broke off, swinging round in his chair, 'We want tea, girl — large quantities of tea — and see that it's properly made and not like dishwater . . .'

'Y — yes, sir,' mumbled the waitress, a little scared, 'shall I bring a pot for two, sir?'

'Bring a pot for *four*,' said Simon Gale. 'We shall then, possibly, be able to squeeze out enough for two. If this were a civilized country one could get beer at this hour. Since, however, it suffers under the petty restrictions of an unimaginative collection of morons, one is forced to curb one's natural inclinations and put up with tea.'

'Yes, sir.' The girl scuttled away, convinced that she was dealing with a madman.

'You know, it's rather a strange coincidence we should have met like this — today,' said Jill. 'You're a great friend of Margaret's, aren't you?'

'Known each other since childhood,' said Gale. 'I remember her when she was all legs, red hair, and freckles. Devilish temper she had even then.'

He rolled up his sleeve, and thrust a hairy forearm under Jill's nose.

'See that scar? Maggie did that — with a penknife — stuck it into my arm because she objected to me calling her Maggie!' He shouted with laughter. 'Didn't stop me, though. I've always called her Maggie. I've always wanted to paint her when she was in a temper, but it never lasted long enough . . . How is she? Is she up in town with you?'

Jill stared at him in astonishment.

'*With* me?' she stammered. 'Surely you — you know?'

'Know?' he demanded, 'know what?'

'You must know — the newspapers . . . '

'Look here,' he cried. 'What the devil are you talking about? Newspapers? I haven't seen one of the scurrilous rags for over eight months. I've been abroad — painting in Italy — only got back this morning . . . '

'Then — then you *don't* know . . . '

'My dear young woman,' said Simon Gale, 'that should be sufficiently obvious from what I have just said. Will you kindly stop dithering in this irritating manner, and tell me what it *is* I don't know?'

'Margaret's in — in prison,' said Jill.

'In *prison*,' shouted Gale. 'Maggie?'

'Shsss . . . ' said Jill. 'Please, Mr. Gale — everybody's looking round . . . '

'I don't care a hundred tinkers' cusses

26

if they're looking triangular!' roared Gale even louder than before. 'They can all turn pink and bust and it wouldn't interest me in the smallest degree. *Why* is Maggie in prison?'

'For murder,' answered Jill.

'Murder — whose murder?'

'My father . . . '

'Hallam, eh?' Gale whistled softly. 'By Saint Michael and all the angels! I always knew that infernal temper of Maggie's would get her into serious trouble one of these days . . . '

'Wait,' she broke in, 'you don't understand . . . '

He made an impatient gesture.

'Of course, I understand . . . I've seen Maggie in a temper too often. What did she do — bash Hallam over the head with a poker or stick him with the bread-knife?'

'He was — poisoned . . . '

'*Poisoned?*' Gale's eyes narrowed and his voice changed. 'Here, that's different. There's something wrong somewhere — *all* wrong. Maggie wouldn't do *that* — she wouldn't poison anyone . . . '

'That's what I'm trying to tell you,' said Jill. 'I don't believe she did . . . '

'Of course she didn't,' he swept away the suggestion and very nearly a vase of flowers as well. 'She's altogether the wrong type. She's capable of killing anybody in a fit of temper, but poison . . . Rubbish, nonsense, balderdash!'

'I think so too, but she's been tried and found guilty . . . the execution is fixed to take place in seven days' time . . . '

'*Execution?*' thundered Gale, to the horror of the people near by. 'Do you mean these blundering, incompetent numskulls are going to *hang* her?'

'Yes,' replied Jill. 'Her appeal was dismissed and they won't even consider a reprieve . . . '

'Good God Almighty!' Simon Gale was genuinely distressed. His beard bristled with indignation. 'Something's got to be done about this — we've got to get Maggie out of this mess . . . ' He glared round the crowded restaurant with malignant ferocity. 'Look here, we can't talk with all these chattering women round us . . . Come along to my studio

28

. . . there's nobody there but my young brother, Martin, and we can talk in peace . . . I want to hear all about this — all about it . . . '

He jumped to his feet almost upsetting the small table.

'But — but the tea . . . ?' began Jill.

'To hell with the tea!' roared Simon Gale. 'Come on — we'll get a taxi.'

He caught her by the arm and almost dragged her out on to the pavement. By great good luck there was an empty taxi passing and he hailed it.

The studio, she discovered, was in Kensington Church Street, an old house wedged in between an antique shop and a tobacconist's. Gale flung a handful of coins at the driver, pushed her up a short flight of steps, thrust a key in the door, and, before she could recover her breath, had rushed her up an old staircase and into a huge, untidy room with great windows and an enormous skylight, which was littered with painting materials, easels, canvases, shelves, filled with books, and massive armchairs grouped round a stove.

She was hastily introduced to a dark-haired, good-looking man, much younger than Gale, who had been reading, and rose in astonishment at the unceremonious disturbance of his peace.

'Pour out some beer, Martin,' shouted his brother, 'Here you are, Jill — you'll find that chair comfortable.'

She was dying for a cup of tea but she didn't like to sugggest it.

Martin Gale, however, when he had brought his brother a huge foaming tankard drawn from a barrel in a corner of the studio, asked her if she would like some tea.

'Oh, yes, please,' she said, gratefully.

'The kettle is boiling,' he said. 'I'll make some.'

Simon took a prodigious draught from the tankard, flung himself down in a chair and began to stuff an old pipe with tobacco.

'Now,' he boomed, 'let's have the whole story.'

They both listened attentively while Jill told them. When she had finished, Martin looked over at his brother.

'Well, I must say it looks pretty hopeless to me,' he said. 'What do you think, Simon?'

'Pour me out some more beer,' grunted Simon, 'and don't be such a confounded young pessimist.'

'*You* don't think it's hopeless, then, Mr. Gale?' said Jill.

'Me? No,' he answered. 'I don't think it's going to be easy — the time element is going to be the greatest handicap — but hopeless? No, I refuse to admit that it's hopeless.'

'But how can you get round the evidence?' demanded his brother, coming back with the re-filled tankard.

'I've no intention of trying,' retorted Gale. 'I don't care a fig for the evidence! I'll agree that it's pretty damning, but I'll back my knowledge of psychology against sufficient tangible evidence to fill the Grand Canyon. I say that Maggie is as incapable of doing what these nincompoops say she did, as I am of perpetrating an atrocity — like *The Stag at Bay*.'

'I'm sure you're right,' said Jill. The tea which Martin had brought her had made her feel better. The weariness had almost gone.

'Of course I am,' said Gale. 'Only a bunch of congenital idiots could possibly imagine otherwise.'

'I'm not disagreeing with you, Simon,' said Martin. 'I think Maggie's innocent but how are you going to prove it? That's what I want to know.'

'By discovering the person who *really* poisoned Hallam, of course,' said Gale.

'Supposing it was an accident?' asked his brother.

'Sheer flaming nonsense!' snorted Simon. 'That's the one thing it couldn't have been, and you'll see why if you take the trouble to use your brains. No mere accident could have left such a perfect chain of evidence against Maggie. That was planned — and very cunningly planned. No — we can wash out accident.'

'What about suicide?'

'I'm certain it wasn't *that*,' put in Jill. 'If you'd known father you'd have understood what I mean. He was afraid of death . . . '

'In any case the same objection applies

to suicide as to accident,' said Gale. 'If Hallam committed suicide he must have done so in such a way as to make it look as though Maggie had murdered him — deliberately, mark you. Did he hate her?'

Jill shook her head.

'No — they were always rowing, of course — they both had fiendish tempers — but I think in his own way he was fond of her — as fond as he could ever be of anyone except himself.'

'There you are, you see?' exclaimed Simon triumphantly. 'It all boils down to this — there's an undiscovered murderer at large in that village of yours, and one of the most dangerous types of murderer too — a poisoner.'

'How are you going to find him — that's the question,' said Martin. 'You've only got seven days — six really, because there's not much you can do today, now. It's not very long, you know, Simon.'

'I know, I know — we've got to work fast. When are you going back to Easton Knoll, Jill?'

'Well, I *was* catching the seven

forty-three this evening . . . '

'Don't. Wait until tomorrow. Is there a train somewhere in the late afternoon?'

'There's one at five seven. It only runs on Saturday . . . '

'That'll do admirably. Can you put us up?'

'Of course,' said Jill. 'I can wire Mrs. Barrett.'

'Good. Do that,' said Gale. 'We'll catch the five seven tomorrow afternoon. We'd better meet at the station . . . '

'If we're going, why not go tonight?' asked Martin. 'Why waste nearly a whole day . . . ?'

'Don't talk such balderdash, Martin. I'm not wasting anything. I'm going to spend tomorrow interviewing Mayhew, the police, counsel for the defence, Maggie — everybody who can tell me anything at all about this wretched business. I want to get hold of all the details I can — every little tiny single one of 'em. I want to go to Easton Knoll thoroughly primed with all the facts.'

'What excuse shall I give for your

coming — just now?' said Jill. 'People will wonder . . . '

'Let 'em,' said Gale. 'The more they wonder and talk about it the better. We're not going to make any secret of it. We're going to kick up a right-royal hell for leather, blazing row about the reason we are there . . . '

'What good is that going to do?' asked Martin.

'Can't you see?' answered Simon, stabbing at the air with the stem of his pipe. 'Our unknown murderer is at present sitting pretty. All his plans have gone on smoothly oiled wheels. He's got rid of Hallam, for some reason best known to himself, and cleverly shifted the blame on to Maggie. She's been con-victed and sentenced and looks like hanging. He's safe, secure, laughing up his sleeve. And then *we* turn up shouting to high heaven that we don't believe a word of it, and *pretending* that we really know something. In an instant his smug sense of security is shattered. All the red lights begin to glow brightly, and he sees danger in large, capital letters. Do you imagine that he's going to sit quietly and *wait* to see what happens? It's not humanly possible . . . '

'What do you think he will do, then?' asked Jill.

'What you, or I, or anybody else would do in the same circumstances,' he answered. 'He'll try and take further precautions to ensure his safety. He won't be able to help himself — he *must* do something. The uncertainty will gnaw and gnaw at his nerves until he has to *make* a move — any move — to reassure himself — and *that's* when we've got him . . . '

3

I

They all three met at the station as arranged on the Saturday afternoon and reached Easton Knoll in time for dinner. Simon Gale had said very little during the journey. They thought he was asleep but he repudiated the suggestion, when Martin made it, and asserted that he had been thinking.

'I've been dying to ask you,' said Jill when they assembled in the long, low-ceilinged drawing-room at Easton Knoll for coffee. 'How did you get on today? Did you see all the people you wanted to?'

'I did,' he replied. 'I've had a most strenuous, if not altogether unproductive day. At the cost of a very severe strain on my temper, I have succeeded in acquiring all the information available concerning Hallam's death. I saw Mayhew, who is a

37

fool, I saw Sir William Fox, the counsel for the defence, who is an even bigger fool, and I saw Superintendent Shelford, who is the biggest fool of all. With what, in the circumstances, I can only regard as abnormal control, I merely informed them of my opinion without using any of the qualifying adjectives which naturally came to my mind!'

'I wish I'd been with you.' said Jill, laughing.

'It was most instructive.'

'Did you see Margaret?'

'Yes . . . poor Maggie,' Gale tugged at his beard, 'she's trying to keep a grip on herself, but her nerves are wearing thin. She looks as if she might crack up at any moment . . .'

'Can you wonder? It must be awful . . . awful . . .'

'I told her not to worry — we'd soon have her out . . .'

Martin grunted.

'I hope you're right,' he said doubtfully.

'We're going to — we've got to,' said Gale. 'Shelford told me that the local man who handled the inquiry before

Scotland Yard was called in, is a person named Frost — Inspector Frost. What sort of man is he? What's he like?'

'Well, he's middle-aged,' said Jill, 'rather on the stout side . . . '

'Hell's bells! I don't want to know what he *looks* like,' exclaimed Simon impatiently. 'Is he one of these mutton-headed, officious chaps, with an exaggerated sense of his own importance?'

'Oh, no — not a bit like that. He's rather nice . . . '

'Do you think he'll be helpful?'

'Yes, I think he would.'

'Good — we may need him.' said Gale. There was a tap on the door and the housekeeper, Mrs. Barrett came in. She was a pale-faced wisp of a woman, with reddish hair going rapidly white.

'If there's nothing more you'll be wanting, Miss Jill,' she said, 'I'll say good night.'

'All right, Mrs. Barrett,' said Jill. The woman was going when Gale stopped her.

'One moment,' he said. 'You know why

we're here, and what we are trying to do, don't you?'

'Miss Jill told me, sir.'

'Do you believe that Mrs. Hallam is guilty?'

'It's not for me to express an opinion, sir.'

'That's the same thing as saying that you do, isn't it?'

The woman hesitated.

'Isn't it?' persisted Gale.

'I don't know how it could have been anyone else, sir,' she answered, and then suddenly: 'Mr. Hallam ought never to have married again ... He brought it on himself ... '

'Why do you say that?' asked Gale quickly.

'There's been nothing but trouble ever since that woman came here ... '

'That's not fair, Mrs. Barrett,' said Jill.

'I'm sorry, Miss Jill, but it's true — you know it's true ... '

'It wasn't all Margaret's fault ... '

'It takes two to make a quarrel, doesn't it?' said the housekeeper. 'Why did your father want to marry again? It was an

40

insult to your mother's memory. He had you — the living image of her — what more did he want? There was no call to bring another woman to Easton Knoll.'

'Were you here with the first Mrs. Hallam, Mrs. Barrett?' asked Gale.

'She was my mother's nurse,' said Jill.

'Oh, I see. So, naturally, you were very fond of her, Mrs. Barrett.'

The housekeeper's face seemed to change. Her faded eyes lit up and a flush came faintly into her pale cheeks.

'I loved her,' she said. 'I loved her . . . she was beautiful . . . the loveliest creature . . . like a flower . . . and so sweet and gentle . . . ' Her voice broke. 'Poor darling — poor, poor little darling . . . ' Her frail body shook with sobs and she turned suddenly and ran from the room.

'Poor old soul,' said Martin. 'You shouldn't have upset her, Simon.'

'She worshipped my mother,' said Jill.

'That's obvious — very obvious,' remarked Gale. 'How old were you when your mother died?'

'I was twelve . . . ' Jill looked surprised at the question.

'How old are you now?'

'Twenty-five.'

'So your mother died thirteen years ago?'

'Yes.'

'Tell me, Jill, how did your mother die?'

There was a silence and then Jill said, in a low voice:

'Why do you ask that?'

'Because I want to know. I'm interested.'

'It — it was an accident . . . '

'What kind of an accident?' he asked.

'She fell . . . from one of the upstairs windows . . . There's a stone-flagged path that runs along that side of the house . . . '

'How dreadful,' muttered Martin.

'How did she come to fall from the window?' asked Simon.

'I don't know — we never knew exactly,' answered Jill. 'She was leaning out — cutting back some creeper that was growing over the window . . . The sills are very low . . . I suppose she overbalanced . . . '

'Where was Hallam when it happened?'

'In his bedroom. He came rushing downstairs — he'd heard her scream — but she was dead — she died almost instantly . . . '

'Why are you so interested, Simon?' asked Martin.

'Because of Mrs. Barrett,' answered his brother slowly.

'Mrs Barrett?' said Jill, frowning. 'I don't understand . . . '

'I should have thought it was obvious. Mrs. Barrett was devoted to your mother — even the lapse of thirteen years has made little difference to her feelings, judging from her behaviour just now. She idolized her in life and still idolizes her memory . . . '

'I still don't see . . . '

'Hell's bells, use your imagination, girl! We're looking for someone with a motive for getting rid of Hallam, aren't we? Well, we've found one person for a start.'

'Mrs. Barrett?' said Martin.

'Of course. Mrs. Barrett worshipped the first Mrs. Hallam to such an extent that even after all this time the mere mention of her produces floods of emotion. People who feel like that about anybody are always potentially dangerous . . . '

'Oh, no — no, it's ridiculous,' declared Jill.

'It's nothing of the sort,' said Gale. 'Listen. Supposing Mrs. Barrett, for some reason or other, gets the idea into her head that *Hallam* was responsible in some way for your mother's death. Wouldn't that give her a motive, eh? She doesn't like Maggie, she resents her coming here in your mother's place — so she kills two birds with one dose of poison.'

'She wouldn't . . . she couldn't . . . '

'I'm not saying she did. I only put it up as an hypothesis to show you how erroneous it is to take even facts for granted. Accepting the basis of my theory as correct, you will see that Maggie was *not* the only person who could have poisoned that whisky and milk. Mrs. Barrett had an equal opportunity, provided that there was any sort of motive. I have supplied her with one — and quite a plausible one too.'

'Very ingenious, Simon,' said Martin with a grimace.

'Naturally!' said Gale.

'I thought you were serious,' said Jill.

'Oh, don't mistake me, I am,' he said. 'After all it might be the truth . . . '

'I should think it was very unlikely,' said Martin.

'It's just impossible,' said Jill.

'Well, we shall see,' remarked Simon Gale. 'Now let's get down to the practical as against theorizing. I want to meet all the people who might be concerned in this and I want to meet 'em as quickly as possible. What do you suggest?'

They began to discuss ways and means . . .

II

The village of Wickham Green boasts a fine old church. It stands in a churchyard surrounded by clipped yews almost as ancient as the building itself. There are tombstones here from which time has erased the inscriptions and there is nothing to say whose bones lie beneath.

It was a fine Sunday morning. The

buds were beginning to break stickily in the horse-chestnuts and the golden blossoms of the forsythias were like yellow wands. The sun was shining from a sky that was almost without a cloud and the twittering of the birds blended with the notes of the organ and the voices of the congregation filing out from inside the church.

Jill Hallam, Simon Gale and Martin, slipped quietly out of the church and stopped a few yards away from the porch.

'I hope it didn't look too bad, Simon,' said the girl, 'leaving before the service was over.'

'Nonsense,' said Gale. 'Only a few people could have seen us. We were right at the back.'

'They must have thought it rather strange, leaving in the middle of the last hymn,' she said.

'Well, it can't be helped if they did,' said Gale. 'We don't want to miss any of the people coming out. This was a brain wave of yours, Martin.'

'It was the obvious thing to do,' said his brother. 'Nearly everybody in an English village goes to church on a Sunday morning. If you want to meet them all quickly, that's the place to be.'

'It's going to save a lot of time,' remarked Simon Gale, 'and time's precious.'

The hymn they could faintly hear came to an end.

'It won't be long before they start coming out now,' said Jill.

Simon Gale looked towards the church porch. His eyes were narrowed slightly.

'It's interesting to think,' he murmured, 'that behind one of these faces we are going to see, may be hidden the mind of a murderer.'

'I wish we could tell which one,' said Jill.

'It would save a lot of trouble, wouldn't it? There should be signs, of course, but very subtle ones.'

'I hope you can spot 'em,' said Martin, 'for Maggie's sake . . . '

'So do I,' said Gale gravely, 'and not only for Maggie's sake — for others as well.'

Jill looked puzzled.

'Others?' she said.

'The poisoner is a very dangerous person, Jill. He doesn't stop at one murder as a rule. He nearly always kills a second time — and a third. It becomes a sort of obsession, you see, until finally it is done almost for *pleasure*.'

The deep notes of the organ began the voluntary and presently the chattering of voices heralded the exodus of the congregation. Almost the first people to appear in the porch were a large, imposing looking woman and a very pretty dark-haired girl whose beauty was marred by a supercilious twist to her mouth and a general expression of supreme boredom.

'There's Mrs. Langdon-Humphreys,' whispered Jill. 'She always manages to be the first one. The girl with her is her niece, Vanessa Lane.'

'She looks a bit of a dragon,' said Martin. 'I don't mean the niece — she looks rather nice . . . '

'Pretty but a little dumb,' said Jill cattily . . . 'Good morning, Mrs. Langdon-Humphreys. Hello, Vanessa . . . '

'Hello, Jill,' greeted the dark-haired girl in a tired, drawling voice. 'Were you in church? I didn't see you.'

'We were at the back,' said Jill.

'The sermon was too long,' said Mrs. Langdon-Humphreys, 'much too long . . . '

'I can't see that it mattered to you how long it was,' drawled Vanessa. 'You were asleep nearly all through it.'

'I always make a point of sleeping through the sermon,' declared Mrs. Langdon-Humphreys. 'What I complain of is that, when it's too long, I invariably wake up before it's over . . . Oh, dear, here comes that tiresome man, Robert Upcott. I did hope we should miss *him* this morning . . . '

'I don't see why,' said Vanessa. 'We've never succeeded in doing so yet.'

A stout, very carefully dressed, little man came mincing towards them. Gale saw with dislike that his flabby cheeks were slightly rouged.

'Good morning, Miss Lane,' he spoke with a slight stressing of his sibilants. 'Good morning, Mrs. Langdon-Humphreys. Isn't it a perfectly wonderful morning, Miss Hallam? Such a pleasure to be alive on a day like this, don't you think?'

'*I* always find it a pleasure to be alive, Mr. Upcott,' declared Mrs. Langdon-Humphreys.

'Of course, of course, dear lady,' beamed Mr. Upcott, 'but the spring, with everything so fresh and clean, just adds that soupçon of delight — that spice to existence. You agree, Miss Hallam — say that you agree?'

'It's my favourite time of the year, certainly,' said Jill. She introduced Simon and Martin who were being favoured with curious stares from the new arrivals.

'Gale?' remarked Mrs. Langdon-Humphreys. 'The name seems very familiar.'

'Are you staying at Easton Knoll?' inquired Vanessa, but looked completely disinterested as to whether they were or not.

'Yes, we came down last night,' said Martin.

'Simon Gale — why, of course!' Mr. Upcott gave a little crow of delight.

'You must be the portrait-painter, my dear sir.'

'Quite right,' said Gale. 'I am . . . '

'I remember now,' remarked Mrs. Langdon-Humphreys. 'I saw something about you in one of the illustrated weeklies, Mr. Gale.'

'Very possibly, Mrs. Langdon-Humphreys,' he answered. 'I frequently appear in the newspapers.'

'My dear sir,' lisped Robert Upcott in a transport of delight, 'this is wonderful! Really a pleasure, a great pleasure to have such an acquisition to our little community. I am an artist myself . . . '

'You paint?' asked Gale.

The little man shook his head.

'No, no, no — I'm afraid I cannot claim any of the creative talents. I meant I was an artist in the sense that I possess an unusual sensitivity to beauty. You will agree — I'm sure you will agree, that beauty is the only thing that makes life worth living . . . '

'I'm not sure that I *do* agree,' said Gale. 'There's a lot to be said for beer and tobacco . . . '

'Oh, my dear Mr. Gale,' Mr. Upcott looked very properly shocked.

'Mr. Upcott collects china, don't you, Mr. Upcott?' drawled Vanessa maliciously.

'Yes — I find it so æsthetically satisfying,' said the little man. 'You must come and see my treasures, Mr. Gale — you and your brother. I have some exquisite pieces — exquisite.'

'That's very kind of you . . . '

'It's so seldom one has the opportunity of discussing these things with someone who possesses a real appreciation of art,' said Mr. Upcott. 'What about this afternoon — come to tea. Could you? Say you *could*?'

To Martin's surprise, who thought that Mr. Upcott was thoroughly unpleasant, Simon accepted.

'We shall be delighted,' he said.

Mr. Upcott was ecstatically pleased.

'Oh, that's really too kind,' he said. 'What about you, Miss Lane, and you, dear lady?'

'I'm afraid not,' said Mrs. Langdon-Humphreys to whom the invitation had been addressed. 'I make it a rule never to go anywhere on a Sunday afternoon.'

'I should like to come,' said Vanessa.

'Splendid,' Mr. Upcott clapped his plump hands. 'Shall we say three-thirty at my little house? I can offer you some really delicious tea — a special blend of souchong . . . '

'We must be going,' broke in Mrs. Langdon-Humphreys. 'Are you staying here long, Mr. Gale?'

'That depends on how quickly we can achieve our object,' answered Simon.

'What is that?' asked Vanessa.

'Well, there's no secret about it,' he said. 'We've come here to find the person who murdered John Hallam.'

There was a sudden and complete change in the atmosphere. The smile on Mr. Upcott's round face became suddenly fixed so that he looked rather like a fat little wax doll. For an instant Vanessa Lane's bored expression disappeared and she looked alert and uneasy. Mrs. Langdon-Humphrey's mouth set and her eyes were suddenly hard.

'You've . . . you've come to do what?' stammered Robert Upcott.

'What do you mean?' demanded Mrs. Langdon-Humphreys regally. '*I* understood that the person had already been found . . . '

'Wasn't it Margaret after all, then?' asked Vanessa.

'No, we don't think it was,' said Simon Gale easily. 'We've found one or two things that make it look as if there had been a mistake.'

'I'm so glad — I always liked Margaret,' said Vanessa.

'What things?' Upcott's voice was tinged with uneasiness. 'What have you found out?'

'You can hardly expect me to divulge that, Mr. Upcott,' said Gale.

'Surely, Mr. Gale, if there is any reason to doubt Mrs. Hallam's guilt,' said Mrs. Langdon-Humphreys majestically, 'it should be a matter for the proper authorities?'

'They don't wish to appear in it yet. The police will, of course, take over later . . . '

'It seems to *me* very unusual,' declared Mrs Langdon-Humphreys.

'Probably,' said Gale, 'but there is a very good reason for it, I assure you.'

'Well, I hope you'll be successful,' said Mrs. Langdon-Humphreys. 'I'm very sorry for Margaret Hallam. Whoever poisoned John Hallam did the world a great service, in my opinion . . . We really *must* go, Vanessa. There's Miss Ginch coming and I will *not* stop here and talk to her. Detestable woman! Goodbye. Come along, Vanessa.'

III

The woman whom Mrs. Langdon-Humphreys appeared anxious to avoid came tripping towards them. She was thin, with slightly protruding upper teeth and a long, drooping nose. Along her upper lip lay a dark line of hair. It was not quite a moustache but very nearly. She was dressed in tweed with a severe, high-necked blouse with a turned down collar and tie. She greeted Jill Hallam in a high-pitched, rather dry voice that was distinctly irritating.

'Good morning, Miss Hallam. Mrs. Langdon-Humphreys seemed in a great hurry this morning, did she not? How do you do, Mr. Upcott.'

Her small eyes darted inquisitively from Gale to his brother and back again.

'Good morning, Miss Ginch,' said Jill shortly.

'Good morning, dear lady,' said Mr. Upcott. 'Busy as a bee, as usual, I perceive.'

'Yes, I mustn't stop a minute,' she answered. 'I'm just taking these to the Vicarage.' She exhibited a parcel of books secured by a strap.

'The dear vicar has so *much* to do. I'm sure that any little help one can give is most welcome.'

'I'm sure you must be invaluable to Mr. Wake, Miss Ginch,' said Jill. 'This is Mr. Gale and his brother, Mr. Martin Gale . . . '

'Oh, how do you do? I saw you in church and wondered who you could be. We see so few strangers, you know . . . '

'The curiosity aroused by strangers in an English village is proverbial, Miss

Ginch,' said Simon.

'Mr. Gale has come here to prove Mrs. Hallam's innocence,' put in Upcott, with his head on one side. 'Incredible, isn't it? *Quite* incredible.'

A startled expression appeared on the rather forbidding face of this unpleasant looking female.

'Oh,' she said, 'Oh, really . . . to prove Mrs. Hallam's innocence . . . indeed . . . I thought it was all settled . . . ?'

'It seems to have given you rather a shock, Miss Ginch,' said Gale.

'Well, naturally,' she compressed her thin lips. 'You see — I thought . . . we *all* thought that it *must* be Mrs. Hallam. Who else *could* it be?'

'Perhaps, you could suggest someone?' said Gale.

'Me? Oh, no, Mr. Gale. Of course, so *many* people hated poor Mr. Hallam, but I don't see how any of them could have had the *opportunity* . . . '

'Did they?' said Gale, quickly. 'That's very interesting . . . '

'Oh, yes indeed,' she hurried on. 'Mrs. Langdon-Humphreys, Major Fergusson,

Doctor Evershed — even the dear vicar disliked him . . . '

'Why?' Gale snapped the question.

'Dear me, I think you'd better ask *Mr. Upcott* that,' replied Miss Ginch, shooting the little man a malicious glance. 'I'm sure he would know better than I would. I really must be running along. I have to leave these books at the Vicarage, you know, and my chickens will be waiting for their little meal. I forgot to give them their breakfast this morning — so *remiss* of me . . . '

'One moment, Miss Ginch,' said Gale, as she was turning away, 'Did *you* hate John Hallam too?'

She caught her breath.

'Oh, no,' she replied. 'I could never be so *wicked* as to hate anyone, Mr. Gale. We are taught to love our neighbours, however great the provocation. I must go to my chickens . . . I can't bear to think of them being hungry, poor things . . . '

She gave a little bird-like nod and tripped away. Robert Upcott looked after her and shrugged his shoulders.

'Fantastic, isn't she? And so *malicious*.

Fancy — just fancy — suggesting that *I* could tell you why people hated Hallam . . . '

'Can't you, Mr. Upcott?' asked Gale.

'My dear fellow, of course not. How *should* I know? I didn't hate the poor man . . . '

The clock in the square tower of the church chimed the quarter and Upcott, almost with a breath of relief, seized the opportunity it offered.

'Good gracious me, is that the time? I mustn't stop here gossiping another second. Don't forget this afternoon. I'm *so* looking forward to it . . . Three-thirty, you know. *Au revoir,* I must positively *rush* . . . '

He beamed on them, waved his hand daintily, and hurried away.

'Hell's bells!' grunted Gale. 'What a dreadful little pansy.'

Jill laughed.

'Poor Mr. Upcott,' she said. 'He was married once. His wife ran away and left him.'

'I don't blame her,' said Martin.

'He's rather sensitive about it,' Jill went

on. 'People laughed — it was rather unkind. She ran away with some man, but nobody ever found out who he was — not even Mr. Upcott.'

'That Ginch woman's a pretty queer specimen,' said Martin, 'something a little mental there, I should think.'

'Repressed spinsterhood, that's all,' said Jill with a twinkle in her eyes.

Simon Gale pulled out his pipe and began to fill it from a disreputable pouch.

'I wonder if that *is* all,' he remarked.

She looked at him quickly.

'You're not suggesting . . . ?' she began.

'No, I'm not,' he broke in. 'Is there a decent pub in this place?'

'There's the *Hand and Flower* in the High Street.'

'Come on then, let's go there,' he said. 'I feel in need of beer — lots and lots of beer . . . '

IV

The *Hand and Flower* was one of those pubs in which you feel instantly at home.

There was nothing elaborate about it. It possessed only one bar, but that was comfortable, with a comfort that more pretentious places of the kind might have envied.

When Jill, Simon Gale and Martin entered the place, the bar was empty. Simon ordered drinks and, when these were brought by the smiling landlord, he swallowed half the contents of his tankard at a draught.

'Ah!' he remarked, smacking his lips, 'that's the best beer I've tasted for a long time. Now, let's see where we've got so far.'

'Not very far, Simon,' said Martin.

'And today's Sunday,' put in Jill, '*Sunday*, Simon. Only *five* more days if we're to do any good . . . '

'I know, I know,' said Gale. 'We've started the ball rolling, anyway. The reason we're here will be all over the village by this afternoon.'

'It was a shock to them, you know,' said Martin. 'They really think we're on to something.'

'That's what we want them to think.

It'll jerk our poisoning friend out of his sense of security . . . '

'Supposing it doesn't? What then?' asked Jill.

'I refuse to suppose anything of the kind,' answered Simon, draining the rest of his beer. 'We're going to pull this off. Get that firmly fixed in your head and keep it there. Hi, landlord — the same again, please.'

'Oh, not for me, Simon,' protested Jill.

'Nonsense, it'll do you good . . . '

'Everybody hasn't your capacity, Simon,' said his brother.

'Drink up and don't argue!' retorted Gale. He pushed his empty tankard across the bar. 'Fill that up to be going on with, landlord . . . '

'Yes, sir,' said the landlord.

'Now listen,' continued Gale, dropping his voice. 'We got on to something very odd this morning . . . '

'Odd?'

'Yes. You must have noticed it. All those people we met had one thing in common — they all disliked Hallam intensely. Why?'

'I'm afraid father wasn't very popular . . . '

'This was more than unpopularity — it was almost hatred. Mrs. Langdon-Humphreys, Upcott, the Ginch woman, Vanessa — they all reacted in the same way when Hallam's name was mentioned.'

'I don't know about Vanessa . . . ' said Martin, doubtfully.

'Oh, yes. She was the same as the others — only she didn't show it so plainly. Upcott was definitely afraid of something — you saw that, didn't you? It was in his eyes . . . '

'When Miss Ginch suggested you should ask *him* why everybody hated Hallam. Is that what you mean?'

'And when he heard why we'd come here. Miss Ginch was as bad as the rest, although she denied it when I asked her point blank. And there are others who felt the same way about Hallam. You remember what she said?'

'I wouldn't take much notice of anything Miss Ginch says,' said Jill. 'She's very spiteful.'

'Women of her type always are,' said Gale. 'She's the ideal anonymous letter writer. Repressed, lonely — watching other people who live normal lives and hating them for it?'

'The same type that breeds the secret poisoner, in fact,' remarked Martin.

'Sometimes. You know, I'm convinced that if we could find the reason why all these people hated Hallam, we'd be well on the way . . . ' He broke off. The door had opened to admit a small, wizened faced, furtive man, roughly dressed and grimy. The landlord, polishing glasses, saw the newcomer and leaned across the bar.

'You can get out, Rigg,' he called, angrily. 'We don't want your kind in here.'

'Why?' demanded the man called Rigg in a surly tone. 'My money's as good as other people's, ain't it?'

'Yer money may be good enough, but you ain't,' said the landlord. 'Now get outside an' don't try an' show yer nose in 'ere again, see?'

'Hell's bells, what's going on?' muttered Gale.

'That's Jonas Rigg . . . ' whispered Jill.

'This is a public 'ouse, ain't it?' said Rigg. 'If I want a pint o' beer an' I've got the money ter pay fer it, I'm entitled . . . '

'You'll get no beer here,' answered the landlord. 'Nor nothing else neither. We don't serve gaolbirds, so the quicker you take yerself off the better . . . '

'It ain't right,' whined the man. 'Just 'cos a chap gets in trouble over a bit of poachin' . . . '

'It weren't that, an' you know it,' said the landlord. 'I wouldn't 'old it against no one fer 'elpin' themselves to a rabbit er two, nor to a pheasant er so, fer that matter. But I won't 'ave thieves in the place, see . . . '

'I never pinched nothin'. It was all lies an' perjury . . . '

'The magistrates give yer three months fer it, any'ow,' said the landlord. 'You're a bad lot, Rigg, an' I don't want you hanging about 'ere, see? Now, clear out afore I come round an' put you out . . . '

'Afraid of upsettin' the gentry, I s'pose?' Rigg's mouth curled in a sneer. 'Huh! *I* don't go around poisonin' people

65

like some I could put a name to . . . '

'That's enough of that,' cried the landlord. 'You get the other side o' the door afore there's any trouble . . . '

'Trouble!' echoed the poacher, and spat. 'I could make trouble enough fer some people, if I'd a mind to. Oh, yes — an' a 'eap o' trouble too . . . '

'Get out!' shouted the landlord. 'Go on, get out!'

He raised the flap of the counter and the little wizened man scuttled to the door.

'Awright, awright, I'm goin',' he snarled. 'You just wait, that's all — just you wait an' see . . . '

He went out slamming the door behind him.

'Nasty specimen,' remarked Simon Gale. 'Sort of local bad character, I suppose?'

'Yes, he lives in a broken-down old caravan near Quarry Wood,' said Jill. 'He's always getting into some trouble or other — poaching mostly.'

'This last seems to have been something more serious,' said Martin.

'It was,' she answered. 'He stole a bicycle from Latt's Farm. He can't have been out of prison long.'

'They gave him three months,' Simon Gale looked suddenly thoughtful. 'Three months,' he repeated slowly. 'When did he steal that bicycle, Jill?'

'When?' She wrinkled her brows. 'Oh, it must have been the night that . . . '

'The night that Hallam was poisoned?' said Gale, sharply.

'Yes, it was,' she looked at him quickly. 'You're not thinking that Rigg could have . . . ?'

'No, but he might have seen something if he was near Easton Knoll that night.'

'What could he have seen?'

'We're assuming that someone came to see Hallam after Maggie had given him that whisky and milk, and gone to bed, aren't we?'

'You mean, Rigg might know who it was?' said Jill.

'I thought he meant Maggie,' said Martin.

'He said: 'I could make trouble enough for some people, if I'd a mind to,'' said

67

Gale. '*That* couldn't have referred to Maggie. Nobody could make any *more* trouble for her. He meant someone else.'

'Simon, I believe we've stumbled on something tangible at last,' declared Martin.

'Yes — I feel that a visit to Mr. Jonas Rigg might be very propitious . . .'

Somebody came quickly into the bar. Jill said in a low voice: 'That's Major Fergusson. Miss Ginch mentioned him . . .'

Gale shifted so that he could see the newcomer. He was a stocky, broad-shouldered man, dressed in plus fours. His face was lean and weatherbeaten but there was a strained look about his rather deep-set eyes.

'I'd like to meet him. See if you can get him to join us,' said Gale.

'I'll try,' said Jill. 'Good morning, Major Fergusson.' she called.

'Good morning, Miss Hallam,' replied Fergusson curtly. His voice was deep with a slight Scots accent.

'Come over here,' said Jill, 'Simon, this is Major Fergusson — Major Fergusson,

Simon Gale and his brother Martin . . . '

'How do you do?' said Simon.

'What'll you have, Major Fergusson?' said Martin.

'That's very kind of ye — I'll have a whisky, please,' said Fergusson.

'The same again, landlord, and a double John Haig,' said Martin to the landlord.

'Comin' up, sir,' said that worthy cheerily.

'I'll not be able to stay very long, I'm afraid,' said Fergusson. 'I only just dropped in . . . '

'We're all going after this,' said Gale. 'It's very pretty round here, isn't it?'

'Aye,' the other agreed, 'there are some lovely spots. Are you staying here?'

'Yes — at Easton Knoll. We came down last night with Miss Hallam.'

'Easton Knoll's a fine house,' said Fergusson.

'A beautiful old place,' agreed Simon. 'I suppose you knew John Hallam?'

The muscles of Fergusson's face seemed to tighten. The expression of the deep-set eyes hardened.

'Aye, I knew him,' he said, shortly.

'It was a terrible thing to have happened, wasn't it?'

'I suppose it was,' Fergusson's eyes flickered over them and then turned to the door. Gale had the impression that he was seeking some means of escape. 'I feel very sorry for Mrs. Hallam.'

'We think there's been a mistake,' Gale continued. 'As a matter of fact that's why we've come down here.'

'You mean — she didn't do it after all?'

'Yes.'

'Is it just something you think, or have you any evidence?'

'Well,' replied Gale, cautiously, 'you can take it that we have a pretty good reason for thinking so.'

'If it wasn't Mrs. Hallam, who have you in mind?'

'I think it would be better if we didn't mention any names at this stage,' said Gale.

'Maybe.' Fergusson rubbed his chin with a shaky hand. 'Well, I'd be glad to see Mrs. Hallam released. I shouldn't like to think of anybody being punished for killing Hallam.'

'Why do you say that?' asked Gale.

'Because if ever a man deserved to die, he did,' answered Fergusson, and there was a bitter hatred in his voice. 'My sympathies are all with the person who killed him . . . '

'You're the second person to say that today,' said Gale.

'You'll find a good many more, I've no doubt.'

'Why, Major Fergusson?' asked Jill. 'Why did everybody dislike my father so much?'

He looked at her sharply.

'Do you not know?' he said. 'Well, it's no business of mine to tell you, I'm thinking. Maybe you'll find out. I don't want to discuss Hallam or anything about him. Good day to you, gentlemen — good day, Miss Hallam.'

He turned abruptly and walked out of the bar.

'Well!' exclaimed Martin with a grimace. 'What's the matter with him? He's left his whisky . . . '

'We rattled him,' said Gale. 'His nerves are in a pretty bad state.'

'He was badly wounded in the war,'

said Jill. 'Something to do with his head. I think it troubles him a lot.'

'I don't think it's *that* that's troubling him,' said Gale. 'I should say he had something on his mind . . . '

'A guilty conscience, eh?' said Martin.

'It might be,' Gale looked doubtful. 'He's not the right type, though, for a poisoner. I can't imagine him killing anyone *that* way, or letting someone else suffer for it, if he had . . . '

'He's definitely another Hallam hater, isn't he?' said Martin.

'The list grows, doesn't it?' Simon swirled the beer in his tankard and took a long drink. 'I wonder how many more we shall find?'

'Doctor Evershed, according to Miss Ginch,' said Jill.

'And the vicar, too,' Gale swallowed the rest of his beer. 'It's the 'why' I want to know. What did Hallam *do* to all these people?'

'I don't know,' she said, shaking her head.

'How far away is Quarry Wood?' he asked abruptly.

'About fifteen minutes walk from here,' she said.

'We've time before lunch, then,' said Gale. 'Finish your drinks and we'll go and find Jonas Rigg. Perhaps he'll have something interesting to tell us.'

4

I

Jonas Rigg's caravan stood in a small clearing on the fringe of the wood. It was a battered and disreputable looking affair, once painted cream, but now a dingy, nondescript colour from dirt and long exposure to the weather. The wheels were broken so that one side of it had had to be propped up on a pile of bricks. Weeds grew thickly underneath, and there was all kinds of rubbish scattered around it.

'Does Rigg live there all the year round?' asked Martin, when they came in sight of the unsavoury looking place.

'I suppose so,' said Jill. 'I've never heard of him living anywhere else.'

'A bit draughty in the winter, I should imagine,' said Simon. 'There isn't a whole pane of glass in any of the windows.'

'The place looks deserted,' said Martin. 'No sign of life anywhere.'

'Perhaps he's inside,' said Gale. 'Let's try the door.'

He mounted the broken steps and rattled the handle.

'It's locked,' he said.

'Try knocking,' suggested Martin.

Simon thumped on the door with his fist, but there was no reply.

'He can't be there,' said Jill.

'No, most likely having been refused beer at the local, he's gone farther afield,' said Gale.

'It's not much good waiting, is it?' she said. 'He may be hours . . . '

'We'll have to come back later,' said Simon. 'Pity. Can you see anything through that window, Martin?'

'No, it's boarded up inside,' answered his brother, craning his neck.

'Now then,' shouted a rough voice angrily, 'what are you doin' there, eh? That's my property, that is.'

They looked round. Jonas Rigg appeared from among the trees and advanced towards them.

'We want a word with you, Rigg,' said Gale.

'I don't want no words with anyone,' snarled the man. 'Go on — you clear off — all of yer . . . '

'There's no need to adopt that tone, my man,' snapped Gale.

'Your man,' retorted Rigg 'Your man? I ain't your man, nor anyone else's man. I'm me own man, an' I'll adopt what tone I like. This is where I live, an' I don't want you or anyone else, snoopin' round . . . '

'I merely want to ask you a few questions,' said Gale.

'Well, you won't get no answers if you does. Go away and leave me alone.'

'Look here, Rigg . . . ' began Gale.

'You look 'ere, mister,' interrupted the man, rudely. 'If I come worryin' round your 'ouse, you'd 'ave me thrown out, wouldn't yer? Well, this is my 'ouse, see, an' I've just as much right to my privacy as what you 'ave . . . '

'I don't want to disturb your privacy,' said Gale. 'If you'll tell me what I want to know, you can have all the privacy you want, and I'll pay for the information into the bargain.'

'Wot d'yer want to know?' demanded Rigg, suspiciously.

'Do you know Easton Knoll?'

'Everybody round these parts knows Easton Knoll,' said Rigg. 'Why?'

'Were you near Easton Knoll on the night that Mr. Hallam was killed?'

' 'Ere, wot are you tryin' to get at?' the man said.

'I'm not trying to get at anything, if by that you mean am I trying to trap you into an admission that may get you into trouble,' answered Gale.

'It don't matter whether you are or you ain't, see,' grunted Rigg. ''Cos I wasn't nowhere near Easton Knoll that night.'

'You're quite sure? It was the night you stole that bicycle . . . '

'I never stole no bicycle neither . . . it was all lies . . . '

'I don't care a tinker's damn if you stole forty bicycles,' said Gale impatiently. 'All I want to know is — did you see anyone in the vicinity of Mr. Hallam's house that night?'

''Ow could I see anyone if I wasn't there?'

'Don't make a mistake, Rigg,' interrupted Jill. 'It's very important. I'll see you're well paid . . . '

'I ain't makin' no mistakes, miss,' answered the man. 'I wasn't there, I tell yer. 'Ow many more times 'ave I got ter say it?'

'That's your story and you're sticking to it, eh?' said Gale.

'You wouldn't want me to tell what ain't true, now *would* yer, mister?' answered Rigg, with a cunning leer.

'No, but I should like to hear you tell me the truth,' retorted Gale.

'Now, see 'ere,' Rigg's voice rose truculently. 'I'm not wastin' time arguin'. I can't tell you nothin' an' that's that.'

Simon Gale looked at him for a moment and then he shrugged his shoulders.

'Oh, very well,' he said. 'Come on you two, let's go.'

Rigg stood looking after them as they walked away, and there was a sneer on his ugly mouth.

'Do you think he was telling the truth?' asked Jill, breaking a short silence.

'No,' said Simon, frowning. 'It's quite evident what his game is. He thinks he'll get more from somebody else, by holding his tongue, than he would from us if he told what he knows.'

'Blackmail?' grunted Martin.

'Yes.'

'But, Simon, that must mean . . . '

'That he *did* see someone at Easton Knoll on the night that Hallam died? I'm sure he did. I think he saw the murderer . . . '

II

Simon Gale was very quiet during lunch that day. He scarcely spoke at all until Mrs. Barrett brought coffee to them in the drawing-room, and then he said, as she was leaving the room:

'Don't go for a minute, Mrs. Barrett, I want to talk to you.'

'Yes, sir?' She waited patiently.

'I expect you remember fairly vividly what happened on the day before Mr. Hallam died?'

'I ought to,' she answered bitterly. 'I've had to tell it often enough. The police, and the lawyers, and then in court . . . '

'Yes, of course . . . Did anybody call that day?'

'Yes, sir, Mrs. Langdon-Humphreys and Miss Lane called in the morning — about eleven o'clock it was. They wished to see Mrs. Hallam. She was in the garden. They waited in here while I fetched her.'

'Had she got her handbag with her in the garden?'

The housekeeper looked surprised at the question.

'Why, no, sir, of course not.'

'Where was it?'

'I don't know. She used to leave it in the room she'd been using — put it down anywhere, she would.'

'I see. Did either Mrs. Langdon-Humphreys or Miss Lane, go upstairs while they were here?'

'I couldn't say. I was busy in the kitchen, sir.'

Gale looked across at Jill.

'Where were you, Jill?' he said. 'You

didn't go up to London until the afternoon, did you?'

'No,' she answered, 'but I went down to the village to do some shopping in the morning. I didn't get back until nearly lunch-time.'

'Did anyone else call that day, Mrs. Barrett?'

'Mr. Upcott came in the afternoon . . . '

'Upcott?'

'Yes, sir. He wanted to see Mr. Hallam, but Mr. Hallam refused to see him . . . '

'Did he go away?'

'No, sir, not at once. He waited in the hope of seeing Mrs. Hallam.'

'Where was Mrs. Hallam?'

'She was out. She went out in a temper after the — the quarrel with Mr. Hallam . . . '

'That was just before I left,' interposed Jill.

'Had you gone before Upcott came?' asked Gale.

'Yes — I'd no idea he'd called that day until now . . . '

'I didn't think it was important enough

81

to mention, Miss Jill,' said Mrs. Barrett.

'Exactly,' broke in Simon Gale. 'You see — that's what happens. People *will* make their own selection as to what is, and what is not, important. Did Mrs. Hallam take her handbag with her?'

'She never did, sir, when she went walking down here.'

'Women don't in the country, Simon,' said Jill. 'Only if they're going shopping.'

'I thought probably she didn't,' he said. 'What time did Mrs. Hallam come back?'

'About six — just before Miss Ginch called . . . '

'Hell's bells!' exclaimed Gale so loudly that the housekeeper jumped. 'Did the entire population of the village call that day? What did Miss Ginch come for?'

'About the sale of work, sir, at the church hall. Mrs. Hallam had promised to look out some things . . . She went upstairs and fetched the parcel for Miss Ginch.'

Gale shot a significant glance at Jill, but he made no verbal comment.

'What sort of relations were Mr. and

Mrs. Hallam on that evening? Still quarrelling?'

'Mr. Hallam was rather silent during dinner, but Mrs. Hallam seemed in quite good spirits.'

'She sounded very cheerful when I rang up to say I was staying in town,' said Jill.

'Did anything else happen that evening?' asked Gale. 'Anybody else call? Anything at all?'

'No, sir, not that I know,' Mrs. Barrett shook her head. 'I went to bed early — just after ten.'

'You didn't hear anything after you'd gone to bed? The sound of voices — a knock at the door — anything?'

'No, sir, I heard nothing.'

'All right,' said Gale. 'That's all I want for now, Mrs. Barrett.'

When the housekeeper had gone he looked at Jill and Martin. He said, pulling out his pipe and filling it:

'You realize what that means, don't you? Any *one* of those people who called that day *could* have got the key from Maggie's bag, and helped themselves to those barbitone tablets.'

'But which of them did?' said Martin. 'That's the question.'

'I don't know, but we're getting somewhere — we're *getting* somewhere . . .'

'I hope so,' said Jill. She looked at her watch. 'In the meanwhile, if we're going to get to Robert Upcott's house by half past three, we'd better hurry . . .'

III

Mr. Upcott came to the door himself. He was beaming with delight and he fluttered round them with a consideration that was most irritating.

'Come in, come in,' he lisped. 'Let me take your coat, Miss Hallam — put your things on the console table, gentlemen. It's such a pleasure to welcome you to my little nest.'

Gale murmured 'that it was very kind of him to ask them.'

'Not at all, not at all, I'm only too *delighted*,' the little man answered him. 'Come into the drawing-room — I do hate the word 'lounge' don't you? So reminiscent of an hotel. The tea's all ready, but I won't make it until Miss Lane arrives. I expect she'll be here at any moment . . . '

Chattering happily he led the way into a long, low ceilinged room that was very tastefully furnished and spotlessly clean and neat.

'What a charming room,' said Jill, and meant it.

'You like it? I'm so glad,' Mr. Upcott clapped his hands in a transport of delight. 'I *do* think it's so important to live amid beautiful surroundings, don't you? I adore my little treasures . . . '

He pointed out some of the best of his pieces and he was in the midst of this when the front-door bell rang.

'That will be Miss Lane,' he said. 'Do excuse me, won't you?'

He tripped quickly away and they looked at each other.

'A bit overpowering, isn't he?' muttered Martin.

'He's got a very good make-up on,' said Jill maliciously. 'And the perfume

— Chanel number five . . . '

Vanessa's drawling voice reached them from the hall.

'I thought I was never going to get here,' she said.

'Oh, you're not really late,' answered Upcott. 'The others have only just arrived. They're in the drawing-room. Will you join them? I'll just slip along to the kitchen and make the tea . . . '

She came into the room languidly.

'Hello, everybody,' she greeted. 'I was afraid I was going to be late. It would have been your own faults if I had . . . '

'Ours, Vanessa?' said Jill inquiringly.

'Yes, the whole village is talking about you,' replied Vanessa, 'you know — about the reason you're here, Mr. Gale.'

'Has it got round already?' said Simon Gale. 'That's pretty quick work.'

'Oh,' she said, 'it doesn't take long for news to spread in *this* place. Miss Ginch started it — she always does, you know? I met several people on my way here, and I thought they were going to keep me talking about it for ever . . . '

'What did they say?' asked Gale.

'They can't see how Margaret can be innocent because . . . '

'Here's the tea,' Robert Upcott minced in with a tray, 'I do hope you will like it. It's a special blend of souchong that I have sent me from London. So wonderfully refreshing. I'm sure you'll *adore* it. Will you pour out, or shall I, Miss Hallam?'

He set the tray down on a low table.

'I'd rather you did, Mr. Upcott,' said Jill.

'Of course, of course, dear lady, if you wish. You all take milk?'

He looked round inquiringly and received affirmative nods.

'Why don't these people, you met, think Mrs. Hallam can be innocent, Vanessa?' asked Gale, bringing the conversation back to the point where Upcott's entrance had interrupted it.

'Well, you see,' said Vanessa, 'they all say Margaret must have done it because nobody else could have put the stuff in that drink. There was nobody else *there* to do it.'

'That's just where you're wrong,'

answered Gale, 'there was. Somebody who called to see John Hallam that night *after* Mrs. Hallam had gone to bed . . . '

'Oh, Mr. Upcott, *do* look what you're doing!' cried Jill. 'You're pouring the tea into that plate of sandwiches . . . '

'Oh, dear, so I am,' Robert Upcott jerked the spout of the teapot up and stared in surprised dismay at the ruined sandwiches. 'Oh, dear me, how — how very stupid of me . . . '

There was a sudden and rather embarrassing silence. They looked at each other uncomfortably and then Simon Gale said:

'What's the matter, Upcott? I don't think even your special blend of souchong will improve the flavour of anchovy sandwiches, do you?'

5

I

Martin Gale came quickly down the stairs into the big hall at Easton Knoll. Somewhere in the house a clock began to strike and he counted the strokes as he made his way to the dining-room. Eight o'clock. Mrs. Barrett was coming out with a tray, as he went in.

'Good morning,' he said cheerfully.

'Good morning, sir,' said the house-keeper.

'Am I first down,' he asked.

'Oh, no, sir. Miss Jill's been up a long time. She's had her breakfast and gone down to the village . . . '

'Oh,' said Martin, 'has my brother gone with her?'

'No, sir, he's in the study, I believe. I'll bring you some fresh coffee.'

'Thank you, Mrs. Barrett.'

The housekeeper went out and Martin

went over to the window and looked out. It was a lovely morning. The sun was shining and there was a filmy veil of green over the bare branches of the trees — almost like a mist — and everything looked fresh and clean. The window was open and Martin drew in great gulps of the sweet smelling morning air. He turned as Jill called to him from the door.

'Hello, Martin,' she greeted. 'Just got up?'

'Yes,' he said. 'You must have got up with the crack of dawn.'

'I did. It was such a lovely morning I couldn't stay in bed. Besides I wrote to Margaret last night, and I wanted to catch the first post . . . '

'Oh, that's where you've been.'

'Yes. Where's Simon?'

'In your father's study so Mrs. Barrett says. What's happening today, do you know?'

'I don't know what Simon's planned. I only saw him for a moment.'

'Was he up early too?'

'Yes — before me,' she answered.

Mrs. Barrett came in with a laden tray.

'Here's your breakfast, sir,' she said.

'Thank you,' said Martin. He sat down at the table. Jill poured out his coffee and when the housekeeper had gone she said:

'Do you realize we've only four more days, Martin — and that's counting today?'

He nodded, his mouth full of bacon and mushrooms.

'I don't see how we're going to do it in the time,' he said. 'Unless he can get that man, Rigg, to talk.'

'We're not even *sure* that he knows anything,' she said.

'Simon thinks he does. Why can't we *make* him say if he knows anything?'

'What do you suggest?' asked Simon Gale, appearing suddenly at the open window. 'Torture?'

'Oh!' exclaimed Jill. 'Simon, you startled me.'

'Sorry,' he apologized, coming into the room. 'I've been for a stroll round the garden. I was just coming in when I overheard what Martin was saying . . . Speaking of torture — that's a queer collection of books in your father's study, Jill.'

'Horrible, aren't they?' she said.

'Most instructive as a sidelight on his character.'

'Why — what are they?' asked Martin.

'*The Life of the Comte de Sade, A History of the Spanish Inquisition* . . . the shelves are full of that sort of stuff . . . '

'Father was always interested in things like that,' said Jill.

'Always?' inquired Simon.

'I never remember him any different,' she answered.

'You weren't very fond of him, were you?'

She hesitated.

'I tried to be,' she replied after a pause, 'particularly after mother died but I could never get *near* him. Do you understand?'

'Yes, I think I do,' he said.

'Sometimes I thought I had,' she went on, 'and then he would say something that hurt — hurt terribly. You knew that he *meant* it to hurt, and — and it sort of froze you up . . . '

'What on earth made Maggie marry a

man like that?' demanded Martin.

'Oh, he could be very charming when he liked,' said Jill. 'He was always courteous in little ways. He might be *saying* hurtful things to you, but he'd never forget to open the door, or give you a chair . . . but he did it with a sneer. Do you know what I mean?'

'Yes . . . ' Simon Gale tapped the stem of his pipe against his teeth thoughtfully. 'I'm beginning to get a pretty good mental picture of John Hallam. It opens up an interesting speculation . . . '

'What's the good of speculation?' said Martin. 'We've got four days — that's all — four days if we're going to save Maggie . . . '

'Hell's bells, I know that!' answered his brother. 'But we're not going to get anywhere by rushing around just for the sake of it. I know what you'd like — you'd like to go and shake the truth out of Rigg, wouldn't you?'

'Well, I think we ought to do *something* about him,' said Martin.

'We'd get nothing out of Rigg that way.

All he's got to do is stick to it that he knows nothing, and we're no better off.'

'What about Upcott?' said Martin. 'That was jolly queer behaviour of his yesterday — pouring the tea into the sandwiches . . . '

'He explained that,' said Jill. 'He said that he was so interested in what Simon was saying that he forgot what he was doing . . . '

'I know he did, but *I* think it was shock,' said Martin. 'He was scared. That remark of Simon's about somebody coming to see your father after Maggie had gone to bed, frightened him. If Rigg saw *anybody* that night, I'll bet it was Upcott.'

'What reason would he have for killing father?'

'What reason would anyone have?' said Simon. 'That's one of the things we've got to find out.'

'There's such a *lot* we've got to find out,' grunted Martin gloomily. 'How can we hope to do it . . . ?'

'Hell's bells,' exclaimed his brother. 'Give it time, Martin, give it time.'

'That's just what we haven't got,' grunted Martin.

'We can't do more than we're doing,' said Gale. 'This isn't a job for action — it's a job for thinking — collecting all the odd little pieces and juggling about with them until we get a picture. I've collected quite a few already — I'm going to try and collect a few more now . . . '

'Where from?' asked Jill.

'Your local man — Inspector Frost. I'm hoping there're one or two things he can tell me . . . '

'Do you mind if I meet you somewhere later?' she asked. 'I must look after things here this morning . . . '

'Why not meet us in the pub?' said Martin. 'I said we'd see Vanessa there about midday . . . '

Jill regarded him coldly.

'Vanessa?' she said. 'I should have thought there was plenty you could do instead of chasing Vanessa about . . . '

'I'm not *chasing* her,' protested Martin. 'I merely suggested we should meet her for a drink . . . '

'And a very good idea, too,' interposed

Simon, with a sharp and understanding glance at Jill's angry face. 'Vanessa interests me. I'd like to know what lies underneath that slightly bored manner she adopts. I'm sure it could be something quite unexpected. There are depths to that young woman which might be very surprising . . . '

Jill said nothing. With a muttered excuse she hurried out of the room, slamming the door behind her with unnecessary force . . .

II

Inspector Frost looked like a farmer. His face was red and shining but the eyes, small and set a shade too close to his rather bulbous nose, were shrewd. He sat behind the desk in his little office and listened quietly and without interruption to what Simon Gale had to say. When he had finished, the Inspector sat back and slowly expelled his breath.

'Well, sir,' he remarked, 'you've flabbergasted me, an' that's a fact. It never

96

struck me there could be any doubt about Mrs. 'Allam's guilt.'

'From your point of view,' said Gale, 'it must have been the obvious conclusion.'

'There wasn't any other, sir,' said the Inspector, shaking his head. 'I still think it's the right one.'

'I'm not asking you to change your opinion,' said Gale. 'All I want is a little help.'

'You can 'ave that, sir, an' welcome,' answered Frost heartily. 'I'd be glad if I could 'elp Mrs. 'Allam, an' that's a fact. A very nice lady, I've always thought her.'

'Good.' Simon took a slip of paper from his pocket. 'Now, I've jotted down some questions I'd like to ask you.'

'Ask what you like, sir. I'll tell you anything I can, though I reckon you're goin' to 'ave all your work cut out to do what you're tryin' to do.'

'I know, but I'm going to do it all the same.'

'Well, I wish you luck, sir,' said Frost.

'Thank you,' said Gale. 'Now, first of all — about this whisky and milk in which the poison was supposed to be administered: could the barbitone have been *already* in either the whisky or the milk which Mrs. Hallam used?'

The Inspector shook his large head.

'No, sir. You can wash *that* out. The remains of both the whisky and the milk she used was analysed, an' there wasn't a trace of anything at all. The poison was put in the mixture *after* she'd made it.'

'There can't be any mistake about that?'

'No, sir. It was all gone into very thoroughly at the time . . . '

'Right. Well, the next thing is this: when you made an examination of the study, after the murder, were the French windows fastened?'

'Fastened an' bolted on the inside, sir.'

'Hallam could have done that himself — before the poison took effect?'

'I s'pose 'e could, sir.' Inspector Frost's eyes suddenly looked very shrewd indeed. 'Is it your idea, sir, that somebody paid 'im a visit that way *after* Mrs. 'Allam 'ad left 'im?'

The Inspector considered this.

Gale nodded.

'Well, I s'pose they could've,' he admitted doubtfully.

'What's more,' said Gale, 'I think the person was *seen* . . . '

'*Seen?*' Frost suddenly became very alert. He leaned forward across the desk. 'Ah, now — if you could prove that, sir, you'd be gettin' somewhere. That'd be evidence . . . '

'Do you know a man named Rigg — Jonas Rigg?' asked Simon.

'I should think I do,' said Frost with disgust in his voice. 'An' no thin' to 'is credit. A thoroughly bad lot if ever there was one. You're not tellin' me . . . ?'

'Would you say he was capable of blackmail?' said Gale.

'I wouldn't put nothin' past Rigg,' declared Inspector Frost. 'As long as it didn't put 'is own dirty skin in danger. What are you . . . ?'

'I think Rigg saw somebody at Easton Knoll on the night John Hallam died,' said Simon Gale.

'An' 'e's blackmailin' this person — is that your idea?' said Frost.

'Yes.'

'Why do you think this, sir?'

'I've talked to Rigg. It's obvious from his manner that he knows something, but although I offered to make it worth his while, he remained as mum as an oyster. There's only one reason for that — with a man like Rigg — he hopes to make more from somebody else.'

Frost nodded his agreement.

'That seems to be pretty sound reasonin', sir,' he said, 'allowin', of course, that 'e really knows anythin'. 'Ave you any idea who this person is?'

'No, not yet.'

'It'd 'ave ter be someone with a motive, wouldn't it?'

'Well, from what I can gather, Hallam was pretty generally disliked.'

'He wasn't what you'd call a popular gentleman,' said the Inspector, 'but that's not a good enough motive for murder, sir . . .'

'That depends . . . Do you know *why* he was unpopular, Inspector?'

'No, sir.'

'I've a vague idea — if I'm right quite a number of people might have a reason for wishing to murder him.' Inspector Frost pursed his lips.

'You'd still 'ave to show that they *could* have done it, sir,' he said. 'What you're going to be up against is the fact that barbitone stuff was kept in Mrs. 'Allam's bedroom in a locked drawer . . . '

'And the key in her handbag,' Gale nodded. 'Yes, I know. What would you say if I told you that at least *five* people had an opportunity of getting hold of that key on the day before Hallam died?'

'I'd say that you'd still 'ave to prove that one of 'em *got* hold of it, sir — an' what's more, that they also took the barbitone . . . '

'I realize that, of course.'

'Who was the five people, sir?'

'Mrs. Langdon-Humphreys, Vanessa Lane, Mrs. Barrett, Robert Upcott, and Miss Ginch.'

Frost frowned at the inkpot in front of him.

'Well, I can't see any of *them* poisonin' Mr. Hallam,' he said. 'Except maybe, Miss Ginch. She's a queer old girl, an' that's a fact. Always smarmin' round the vicar, poor chap, an' runnin' everybody else down be'ind their backs. The lies she tells about people — you'd never believe it. Doctor Evershed threatened 'er with an action once for the things she said about 'im . . . '

'Ah, yes, Doctor Evershed. I haven't met him yet. What's he like?'

'Very nice chap,' declared the Inspector, 'a bit abrupt in his manner, an' there's some as don't like 'im at all. But 'e's a clever doctor. He bought old Doctor Croxton's practice when he retired a couple o' years ago . . . '

'He's practically a newcomer, then?' said Gale.

'Yes.'

'What did Miss Ginch say about him?'

'It was about one of his patients — a woman. He's a good-lookin' feller an' youngish for a G.P. in a place like this — about forty, I should say. Miss Ginch started a rumour . . . well, you know the sort of mush, sir?'

'Presumably Miss Ginch had tried her charms on Doctor Evershed without success, eh?'

A deep rumble shook the large bulk of Inspector Frost. Simon Gale gathered that he was chuckling, though there was no change in the expression of his face.

'I expect you're about right there, sir,' he said. ''As a go at every man, she does, an' ud run a mile if any of 'em took any notice of 'er.'

'I suppose it was Doctor Evershed who was called in when Hallam was found dead?'

'Yes.'

'And was he the first to notify the police that there was something wrong?'

'Yes, sir.'

There was a short silence, and then Simon folded up his notes and put them in his pocket.

'Well, I think that's all for the time being,' he said. 'If I want any help, I can count on you, can I?'

'You can, sir,' said Frost, and added: 'so long as it's in an unofficial capacity.'

'Of course, that's understood. All the same if you *should* hear of anything . . . ?'

'I'll let you know at once, sir.'

They shook hands. As Gale was going

out of the door, Frost said: 'I *might* make one or two inquiries — along the lines you mentioned — strictly in my spare time, of course . . . '

'I'd be very grateful,' said Simon. 'Goodbye, Inspector . . . '

'Good mornin', sir — an' good luck . . . '

III

Simon found his brother waiting for him outside the little rural police-station.

'Hello,' said Martin. 'You've been a deuce of a time. Why didn't you let me come in with you?'

'Because I thought it would be better to see him on my own.'

'How did you get on? What sort of chap is he . . . ?'

'Very amiable . . . Hell's bells, look who's bearing down on us . . . '

Martin looked round. The thin form of Miss Ginch was crossing the road and coming towards them with deadly intent. There was no possible way of dodging her so they had to make the best of it.

'Good morning, Mr. Gale,' said Miss Ginch, gushingly. 'How are you, and how is your brother? Didn't I see you come out of the police-station just now?'

Her expression dared either of them to deny it.

'I've no doubt you did if you happened to be looking in that direction,' said Gale.

'I was sure I wasn't mistaken,' said Miss Ginch. 'Do tell me, Mr. Gale, are there any new developments? When is Mrs. Hallam going to be released? I'm so anxious about it all. I always felt there was a mistake, you know . . . '

'Did you Miss Ginch? I rather gathered yesterday that you . . . '

'Oh, yes,' said Miss Ginch, speaking very rapidly. 'I couldn't imagine dear Mrs. Hallam doing such a dreadful thing. You're a very great friend of hers, aren't you, Mr. Gale?'

'Yes, we were almost brought up together . . . '

'How very extraordinary.'

'Why should it be extraordinary?' asked Martin, in surprise.

'It seems to me so peculiar that you've

never been here *before*,' said Miss Ginch, meaningly. 'If you and Mrs. Hallam were such friends I should have thought you would have come to visit her. But, perhaps, the friendship did not extend to *Mr. Hallam*?'

'It didn't,' said Gale, shortly. 'I never met him.'

Having shot her shaft, Miss Ginch proceeded happily:

'Such a strange man, Mr. Gale. Yes *indeed. I've* always felt so *sorry* for Mrs. Hallam and Jill. Poor things! So difficult to have to *live* with anyone like *that*, you know?'

'Like — *what*, Miss Ginch?'

'Well, not a very *nice* person, I'm afraid,' said Miss Ginch making strange noises with her teeth. 'Oh, no, *not* a nice person at *all* . . . not at all . . . '

'Look here, Miss Ginch,' said Simon, bluntly, 'what do you mean? People keep on hinting at something peculiar about John Hallam, but nobody comes out into the open and says what it was . . . '

'Well, of course, it's only what I've *heard*,' said Miss Ginch cautiously. 'I do think people should be careful of repeating *gossip* — they get into such *trouble,* you know. You should ask Mr Upcott or Major Fergusson, or Mrs. Langdon-Humphreys . . . '

'Here's Upcott now,' interrupted Martin.

'Oh, dear,' said Miss Ginch, very flustered with a spot of colour staining her yellow cheeks. 'That's Doctor Evershed with him. One always meets everybody in the High Street of a morning . . . Do excuse me — I must be getting on with my shopping . . . Goodbye, goodbye . . . '

She turned hurriedly and tripped away.

'What made her rush off like that?' asked Martin.

Simon Gale chuckled.

'Doctor Evershed, I imagine,' he said. 'Miss Ginch is not very popular in that direction . . . Good morning, Upcott.'

'Good morning, Mr. Gale, good morning,' said Upcott, beaming at them. 'This is quite an unexpected pleasure. Do you know Doctor Evershed? I don't think you do, do you? Doctor, this is Mr. Simon

Gale, the portrait painter — I'm *sure* you must have heard of him. Mr. Gale has come down here to . . . '

'I know,' broke in Doctor Evershed, curtly, 'I've heard all about it.'

'Marvellous, isn't it, how quickly news travels in our little community?' said Mr. Upcott.

'Not while there are people like Miss Ginch in existence,' said Evershed. He was a thick-set, swarthy-faced man. His hair was very dark and he had a full-lipped mouth and rather large brown eyes. Gale thought he looked as if there was a touch of the Latin about him.

'Poor Miss Ginch!' Upcott gave a little high-pitched cackle. 'Our general information bureau, you know, Mr. Gale — not always very reliable, I'm afraid.'

'A thoroughly spiteful and dangerous old gossip,' said Evershed.

'But nobody takes anything she says seriously, Evershed,' said Upcott, quickly. 'You agree — I'm sure that you agree? We all know our Miss Ginch, eh? What particular choice piece of scandal was she discussing with *you*, just now, Mr. Gale?'

'Well, it concerned you,' said Simon, not entirely truthfully.

'Me?' Mr. Upcott looked a trifle uneasy. 'Good gracious, what could she possibly have to say about *me*?'

'She suggested that you know a great deal more about John Hallam than you've admitted . . . '

'Oh, really, this is *too* much,' declared Upcott, 'Quite, quite absurd, of course. I knew nothing about Hallam — nothing at all . . . '

'I understand that you called to see him at Easton Knoll on the day before he died,' said Gale. 'Is that right?'

'Yes, yes, I think I did. But, my dear fellow, why shouldn't I?' Mr. Upcott spread his plump hands. 'There was nothing in it. I'd heard that Hallam had an early Doctor Wall teapot — a very fine specimen — and I was anxious to purchase it for my little collection . . . '

'Did you get it?'

'No,' Upcott shook his head sadly. 'Hallam sent a message to say that he couldn't be disturbed. So *vexing* after going all that way. I suppose he was gloating over one of those horrid books of his . . . Oh, you know about them, do you?'

'Everybody does,' said Doctor Evershed. 'Hallam had a queer streak. Definitely a pathological case, in my opinion.'

'It's rather interesting you should think that, Doctor Evershed,' said Gale.

'He wasn't mad, of course, but close to the border-line,' said Evershed.

'A sort of sadistic obsession — is that what you mean?'

'You understand, eh?' Evershed flashed him an appreciative glance.

'Yes,' said Gale. 'I'd formed the same opinion.'

'Clever of you,' said Evershed. 'Not a unique case, you know. Lot's of 'em about.' He looked at his watch. 'I must be pushing off. Quite a few patients to see.'

'I should like to have a chat with you sometime soon,' said Gale.

'Glad to. After surgery's the best time. Drop round this evening — seven-thirty.'

'Thanks, I will.'

'Goodbye, Doctor,' said Upcott, 'thank

you so much for the prescription.'

Evershed nodded curtly and hurried away.

'My poor nerves are really in a shocking state,' sighed Upcott. 'You know what they were like yesterday? I suffer from insomnia, you know? I simply *had* to go to Doctor Evershed this morning and ask him to give me something. Sleeplessness is dreadful, isn't it? You agree — I'm sure you agree?'

'Never suffered from it,' said Gale. 'I always sleep like a log. What did Evershed give you?'

'Oh, he always gives me the same thing — barbitone tablets. They're *so* efficacious. I shall sleep like a child tonight. Bye, bye — I really *must* run along now . . . '

Martin pursed up his lips in a silent whistle.

'Barbitone!' he said, softly.

Simon Gale nodded.

'Yes — a queer coincidence, isn't it?'

'He's had them before, too.'

'They're quite often prescribed for insomnia.'

'It looks very queer to me,' said Martin. 'Taken in conjunction . . . What are you looking at, Simon?'

'Jonas Rigg. All the time we've been talking he's been watching us . . . '

'I can't see him . . . '

'He's hiding himself in that little passage between those cottages . . . Walk slowly up the street, Martin . . . '

A little bewildered Martin obeyed. Simon strolled along beside him. Presently he said:

'Stop at this shop, and look in the window. Rigg is following us. Let's give him a chance to catch up with us . . . '

They stopped outside the little general stores, and looked in at the assortment of goods in the small window. Footsteps came hesitantly up behind them and stopped.

'I say, mister,' said a voice in a hoarse whisper.

Gale looked round. Rigg was shuffling from one foot to the other nervously.

'What do you want, Rigg?' he asked.

'You know what we was talkin' about yesterday?' said Rigg, his small eyes wary and alert. 'Could you come to my caravan — sometime tonight. I might 'ave somethin' to tell yer . . . '

'Why not tell me now?'

'Not 'ere — I don't want ter be seen talkin' to yer . . . '

'You've changed your tune since yesterday, haven't you. Why?'

'I've been thinkin' . . . I wouldn't like no one to get in trouble fer what they didn't do, see . . . '

'You mean Mrs. Hallam?'

'I ain't mentionin' no names . . . It ud be worth somethin' fer the information, wouldn't it?'

'That depends what it is,' said Gale. 'If it helps to clear Mrs. Hallam I'll see you're all right . . . '

''Ow much, mister?' said Rigg greedily.

'We'll talk about that when I've heard what you've got to say.'

'It'll be worth a good bit — what *I* can tell yer, mister. You come along at eight-thirty, see.'

'All right — I'll be there,' said Gale.

'Don't go sayin' nothin' to nobody, mister, or it's all off, see,' said Rigg, 'an' bring plenty o' cash with yer . . . '

He looked quickly up and down the street and shuffled quickly off.

'What a bit of luck, Simon,' exclaimed Martin. 'So he really did see something. Do you think . . . '

'I think,' said Simon, 'that we'd better hurry up and make for that pub. We promised to meet Jill and I want some beer . . . '

'Lord yes,' said Martin, 'and Vanessa. Let's get a move on . . . '

'Don't say anything about Rigg in front of Vanessa,' warned his brother. 'It will be better if we keep that amongst ourselves . . . '

6

I

Jill and Vanessa had already arrived when they reached the Hand and Flower.

'We'd given you up,' said Jill.

'I was just going,' drawled Vanessa. 'I've got to meet auntie at a quarter to one. You're awfully late . . . '

'We couldn't help it,' said Martin. 'We ran into Upcott and Miss Ginch in the High Street.'

'How dreadful!' Vanessa shuddered. 'They're bad enough singly — together they're perfectly appalling!'

'We also met Doctor Evershed,' said Simon. 'He was with Upcott.'

'Not from choice, I'm sure, Simon,' said Jill. 'Doctor Evershed can't bear Mr. Upcott.'

'No, Upcott had been to see him about his nerves . . . '

'Poor little man!' said Vanessa. 'I don't

like him, but I *do* feel sorry for him.'

'Why?' asked Martin.

'You've heard about his wife running away with some man or other, haven't you?' she said, languidly.

'I told them,' said Jill.

'Well, ever since then, he seems to have gone to pieces — all jumpy and dithery — like he was yesterday afternoon. He never used to be as bad as that, did he, Jill?'

'No.'

'And recently he's got worse,' went on Vanessa. 'Sometimes he looks positively ghastly. I can't think what can be the matter with him.'

'He was genuinely upset at his wife leaving him,' said Jill.

'I can't imagine Upcott married,' said Martin. 'It seems all wrong.'

'It *is* all wrong, of course,' said Vanessa. 'He ought to have remained a spinster!'

They all laughed.

'Vanessa, you shouldn't say things like that,' said Jill.

'Well, that's what he should be,' answered Vanessa. 'He and Miss Ginch are terribly alike, you know — really the only difference is that *he* isn't spiteful . . . '

'I think that's really unkind . . . '

'But it's true,' insisted Vanessa.

'That reminds me, Jill,' said Simon, 'have you got an early Doctor Wall teapot at Easton Knoll?'

She stared at him in astonishment.

'What on earth's that, Simon?' she asked.

'It's rather a rare piece of china, I believe.'

'I don't know,' she answered, 'I'll ask Mrs. Barrett . . . '

'Simon means that thing in the study,' said Vanessa, 'in the corner cupboard by the window.'

'Oh, *that*,' exclaimed Jill. 'Why did you want to know, Simon?'

'It must have got something to do with Mr. Upcott,' said Vanessa.

'China and Upcott do go together, don't they?' said Gale.

'Is it a clue?' asked Vanessa. 'You know everybody's getting terribly excited wondering who it can possibly be if it isn't Margaret?'

'Their curiosity may be satisfied sooner

than they expect,' answered Gale. 'Perhaps sooner than *one* of them will like . . . '

'It's awfully interesting,' she said, 'trying to think who it might be . . . '

'Not quite so interesting for Maggie, you know,' said Gale. 'Her life depends on it.'

Vanessa flushed.

'Oh, I'm sorry . . . I didn't think . . . '

'All she can do is to sit and wait,' he went on relentlessly. 'Can you imagine what it's like that waiting? Going to bed at night and waking in the morning — each day bringing her nearer to — the last morning?'

'Don't,' whispered Vanessa, white to the lips, 'please don't . . . '

'I don't think you'd find it 'awfully interesting' Vanessa,' he said.

She looked as if she were going to cry but she fought back the tears. With a quick movement she swallowed her drink and set down the empty glass.

'I must go,' she said, speaking with difficulty. 'I *must* go . . . I don't — I don't want to keep . . . my aunt waiting . . . '

She walked hastily to the door and went out.

'You shouldn't have upset her like that Simon,' said Martin reproachfully.

'Why not?' demanded his brother. 'It won't hurt her to feel a little human emotion. I thought under all that nonsense she might be capable of it, but I wasn't sure.'

He took a long drink of beer.

'Simon,' said Jill, wrinkling her forehead, 'how did she know about the teapot?'

'What do you mean, Jill — how did she know? She must have seen it.'

'Yes, but when?'

'Oh, sometime when she was in Hallam's study . . . '

'That's just it, Simon,' said Jill. 'So far as I know, she's never been in father's study . . . '

II

There was a knock on the cell door. One of the wardresses got up, went over and unlocked it.

119

'Good afternoon, sir,' she said. 'Here's the chaplain to see you Hallam.'

Margaret Hallam looked up. She liked the chaplain. He was a youngish man, fresh complexioned, and going slightly bald, and he talked humanly.

'Good afternoon, Mrs. Hallam,' he said. 'I've brought you those books I promised.'

He laid them down on the table.

'Thank you,' she said, tonelessly, 'but I don't think — I want to read.'

He pulled up a chair, sat down, and offered her a cigarette. She took it mechanically and he flicked a lighter into flame and lit it for her.

'I'll leave them with you in case you should,' he said. 'It's good to occupy the mind with something, you know.'

'I've plenty to occupy my mind,' she said.

'Have you heard anything from your friends?' he asked.

'There's hardly been time yet, has there?' she said.

'No, I suppose not,' he agreed. 'If there's anything I can do to help in any way, you've only got to ask me, you know.'

'You're very kind,' she said.

'No, no . . . just doing my job.' He sighed. 'I only wish I could do more . . . '

'There isn't very much anyone can do,' she said, 'except to find out the truth . . . '

'Mrs. Hallam,' he leaned across the table, 'you've told me what your friends are attempting to do, and I sincerely hope that they will be successful. At the same time you must realize how difficult the task is that they have undertaken . . . '

'Yes, I know,' she said.

'I only want to warn you,' he went on, 'not to put too much reliance on . . . '

'Oh, I know, I know,' she broke in. 'I'm hoping for a miracle . . . '

' "The most wonderful thing about miracles is that they sometimes happen",' he quoted, 'G. K. Chesterton wrote that . . . '

'I hope he's right in my case . . . ' she said.

'That rests with God, Mrs. Hallam,' he answered. 'We can only do our best. The final decision is with Him.'

'That . . . doesn't make it any easier, I'm afraid . . . '

'No, I can understand that,' he said, quickly.

'Not when you know that each minute — each time the clock strikes — is hurrying you nearer to — to the time when there will be — no more minutes . . . '

'That time is bound to come for everybody, Mrs. Hallam,' he said.

'But they don't know the day, the hour, the actual second, and have to watch it getting nearer and nearer . . . they don't have to live with *that* for weeks before . . . '

'I know. That is an ordeal mercifully spared the majority of us,' he replied. 'I doubt if many of us could face it. To do so requires great courage . . . '

'It's like a line drawn through the middle of your life,' said Margaret. 'A thick black line — and beyond the line . . . there's nothing more . . . '

III

The clock on the mantelpiece in the drawing-room at Easton Knoll struck eight. Simon Gale looked up from a silent contemplation of the fire, took the pipe from his mouth and said:

'It's nearly time we were starting. It'll take half-an-hour to get to Rigg's caravan from here, won't it, Jill?'

'About that, Simon,' she answered. 'There *is* a short cut, but I don't think we'd better risk it in the dark.'

'I hope when we get there, Rigg hasn't changed his mind again,' said Martin.

'I don't think you need worry about that,' said Gale. He got up and stretched himself.

'Why do you think he suddenly decided to tell us anything?' asked the girl.

'Because he was too scared to go through with his original plan,' said Simon.

'Scared?'

'Yes. His first intention was obviously blackmail — that's why we couldn't get anything out of him yesterday — and then he got frightened. He won't get so much out of us, but at least it's — *safe* . . . '

'I wonder what frightened him?' said Martin.

'I think he guessed that the person who poisoned Hallam wouldn't stand for blackmail,' replied Gale. 'It's easier to kill the second time, you know . . . ' He knocked his pipe into the grate. 'We *must* be going — come along . . . '

'I'll just get my coat,' said Jill, 'I won't be a minute . . . '

'All right — hurry up,' he said.

'We'll wait for you in the hall,' said Martin.

It was a dark night with a chill wind. They set out from Easton Knoll, walking briskly to keep warm. The wind had changed since the morning and was almost due north with a consequent lowering of the temperature.

'I say,' said Martin, suddenly remembering. 'Weren't you supposed to see Evershed this evening?'

'I rang him up before dinner and put it off,' said Simon. 'This is the turning, isn't it, Jill?'

'Yes, we haven't very far to go now . . . '

'Good,' grunted Martin. 'I'm frozen . . . '

They turned into the narrow lane which sloped steeply down to Quarry Wood.

'Mind how you go,' warned the girl, 'the road's very bad . . . '

'This isn't the way we came before,' said Martin.

'We came from the 'Hand and Flower' then,' she said. 'This is the best way from Easton Knoll. Rigg's caravan is only a few hundred yards from the end of this lane . . . '

'There's somebody coming,' broke in Gale. 'Look — that's the red tip of a lighted cigar . . . '

It was coming jerkily towards them — a tiny glow in the darkness.

'It must be Major Fergusson,' said Jill. 'He always smokes cigars . . . '

'What on earth's he doing here?' muttered Martin.

'He often goes for long walks in the evening,' said Jill.

The red glow of the cigar came nearer. Presently they could dimly distinguish the figure behind it.

'Good evening, Major Fergusson,' said Gale.

There was a startled exclamation and then Fergusson's voice said:

'Who's that . . . Who are you?'

'Simon Gale — don't you remember? We met in the pub yesterday . . . '

'Ah, yes.' Fergusson was level with them now, and he stopped. 'I could not recognize you in the dark. That's Miss Hallam, isn't it?'

'Yes, it's me,' said Jill.

'You startled me,' Fergusson went on rapidly, 'I didn't expect to meet anyone round here . . . '

'Neither did we,' said Gale. 'Not a very pleasant night to be out . . . '

'The weather makes no difference to me,' answered Fergusson. 'I like walking at night. I find I sleep better. You seem to like it yourselves.'

'Ah, we're not out for pleasure,' said Gale. 'We're on our way to see Rigg . . . '

'Rigg?' exclaimed Fergusson, and he

126

sounded startled, 'you mean Jonas Rigg?'

'Yes.'

'You'll have your trouble for nothing, I'm thinking.'

'Why?' asked Jill.

'I passed his caravan a wee while back and there was no light,' said Fergusson. 'Well, I'll not be keeping you. Good night.'

He walked briskly past them and disappeared in the darkness.

They continued on their way, came to the end of the lane, and presently to the edge of the wood where Rigg's caravan stood.

'Major Fergusson was right,' said Jill. 'There isn't a light . . . '

'I hope Rigg isn't going to let us down,' said Martin.

'It's only just half-past eight,' said Gale. 'He may not have got back yet.'

'Unless he blocks up his windows,' suggested Martin.

'The place is so dilapidated, I should think you would be bound to see a chink somewhere . . . '

They walked over to the caravan. It was

dark and quite silent. Simon Gale went up the steps and tried the door. It opened under his hand, but there was no light inside.

'I don't think he can be here, unless he's asleep,' he said. 'It's too dark to see anything . . . '

Martin joined him.

'Hold on,' he said, 'I'll strike a match, Simon . . . '

He took out a box of matches, struck one, and shielded the flame with his hand. The feeble light shed a faint glimmer round the dark interior of the caravan and:

'Hell's bells!' exclaimed Simon Gale.

'What's the matter, Simon?' called Jill sharply from the foot of the steps.

'See if there's a lamp anywhere,' snapped Gale. 'we must get a light . . . '

She came quickly up the steps.

'There's one on the shelf — in the corner . . . ' she said.

'I see it,' said Martin. 'Wait a minute . . . I'll strike another match . . . '

'Simon,' said Jill, 'is something wrong . . . ?'

'I think there's something very wrong,'

he answered. 'Don't move until we get a light, Jill . . . '

A flame flared up inside the caravan, there was a clink of glass and it began to burn steadily.

'There,' grunted Martin, 'now we can see what we're doing . . . '

'What do you mean Simon,' persisted Jill, urgently. 'What *is* the matter?'

'Rigg's here,' answered Gale, 'but I'm afraid he's dead.'

She gave a little cry.

'*Dead?*' exclaimed Martin.

'Yes . . . '

'Oh,' said Jill, 'oh, no — he can't be . . . '

Simon touched the motionless figure in the chair by the table.

'He is — there's no doubt of it,' he said. 'He's been dead for some time, I think . . . '

'But how — how did it happen?' she demanded, peering it from the doorway.

'I don't know yet. Stay where you are, Jill, and don't touch anything . . . Martin, go and find Doctor Evershed and bring him here as quickly as you can. Get hold of Inspector Frost, too, if you can find him . . . '

'Inspector Frost?' repeated Martin.

'Don't you realize,' said Gale impatiently, 'that this is too *convenient* to be a coincidence . . . '

'Convenient?' said Jill.

'Rigg was going to tell us something tonight — and he's dead . . . '

She caught her breath.

'Simon!'

'Somebody was afraid, Jill. They had to take — precautions . . . '

'Do you mean — it was murder?' asked Martin.

'Of course it was,' asserted Gale. 'I told you that a person who has killed once will always kill a second time — if necessary, didn't I? It became necessary — with Rigg . . . '

'Because — he knew?' whispered Jill.

'Yes.'

'How was . . . how was he killed?'

'I think he was poisoned,' answered Simon Gale.

IV

It was an hour later:

Inspector Frost, his ruddy face grave, edged closer to Doctor Evershed as he straightened up from the body of Jonas Rigg.

'Well, doctor, what do you say? Was it poison?' he asked.

'Yes, there's no doubt of it . . . '

'You *were* right, Simon,' whispered Jill.

'I was certain of it. What was the poison, doctor?' asked Gale.

'One of the hypnotics.'

'Such as — barbitone?'

'Could be barbitone. There's marked cyanosis. Can't say for certain until after the post-mortem.'

'It's horrible — horrible,' muttered Jill.

'Why don't you go home?' Simon swung round on her. 'Let Martin take you . . . '

'No,' she said. 'I'd rather stay . . . '

'You can't do any good here,' said Evershed.

'Come along, Jill,' said Martin. 'I'll go with you . . . '

'No,' she said, stubbornly. 'I'm staying. I want to know . . . '

'Well, so long as Inspector Frost doesn't mind,' said Gale, shrugging his shoulders.

'I don't mind, sir,' said Frost, 'only I think 'ud be better for the young lady if she went, an' that's a fact. We'll be 'ere for a good bit yet . . . '

'I'll wait, Inspector . . . '

'All right, miss, 'ave it your own way,' said Frost good-naturedly, 'Now then — about this poison. What d'you think he took it in?'

'I think it was in the beer,' said Gale. 'That empty bottle was on the table when we found him.'

'The dregs should tell us if you're right,' said the Inspector. 'I'll 'ave 'em analysed. 'Ow long would you say Rigg had been dead, doctor?'

'Two or three hours,' answered Ever-shed, 'Can't be more definite than that . . . '

'These — what-d'you-call-'em — 'ypnotics — are things people take to make 'em sleep, aren't they?'

'That's one of their uses.'

'That kind of stuff 'ud take a fair time to act, wouldn't it?'

'Do you mean before death ensued?'

'Yes — 'ow long would 'e live after swallowin' the stuff?'

'That would depend on the drug and the quantity taken.'

'I'm tryin' to get some idea of the time 'e must 'ave taken it, doctor,' explained Frost.

'Can't help you until I know how much he took,' said Evershed.

'Would you say,' asked Gale, 'that Rigg died from the same kind of poison as John Hallam?'

'It's possible. The symptoms are very similar.'

'So is the method,' said Gale significantly. 'Whisky and milk in one case — beer in the other . . .'

'Now, just a minute, sir,' broke in Frost, 'you're going too fast, an' that's a fact. There's no evidence to show that Rigg was murdered. It could've been suicide . . .'

'It could — but do you think it's

likely?' demanded Simon Gale. 'Rigg had made an appointment to see me. He was going to tell me something that he knew about the murder of Hallam, and he expected to be well paid for the information. Why should he suddenly decide to kill himself? It's all wrong.'

'Are you suggesting that he was killed to stop him talking,' asked Evershed.

'Yes — by the same person who killed Hallam . . . '

'That'd mean that Mrs. 'Allam is innocent,' interpreted Frost.

'Hell's bells,' cried Simon, 'that's the whole point — of *course* she is.'

'Doesn't this *prove it*?' asked Jill. 'Surely this will be sufficient to make them postpone the execution while the police make further inquiries?'

'No, Miss 'Allam,' said the Inspector. 'I'm afraid it won't. You see, there's nothing to connect this with Mr. 'Allam's murder . . . '

'But that's ridiculous,' exclaimed Martin. 'Rigg was going to tell us something about Hallam's murder . . . '

'Yes,' said Jill, 'and he was killed in the

same way — with the same poison.'

'Maybe, but there's still no real evidence, miss,' said Frost. 'Rigg was goin' to tell you somethin'? All right — *what*? You *think* it was somethin' to do with 'Allam's murder. You *think* 'e saw someone at Easton Knoll that night . . . '

'I'm convinced he did,' said Gale.

'An' I'm prepared to agree with you, sir. I think there may be a lot in what you've told me, but it don't rest with me, an' that's a fact. It's the 'Ome Office that's got to be convinced, an' they'd pooh-pooh the whole thing . . . '

'They can't pooh-pooh Rigg's death. That's a fact . . . '

'Yes, sir, but they'll say that Rigg copied the way Mr. 'Allam 'ad been killed in order to kill himself, or that somebody had copied it in order to kill 'im . . . '

'You're right,' said Evershed. 'He's right you know.'

'We can't tell 'em anythin' that 'ud help Mrs. Hallam, an' that's a fact,' declared Frost.

'If only Rigg had told us what he knew,' said Martin.

'I blame myself for that,' grunted Simon. 'I should have stuck to him until I'd got it out of him. I ought to have foreseen that something like this would happen . . .'

'Oh, come now, sir,' said the Inspector, 'I don't see 'ow you could've done that . . .'

'Because I knew there was a murderer at large,' said Gale, 'that's why. A clever, cunning murderer who'll do anything to keep hidden and — safe.'

'It's frightening,' said Jill, 'to think that somebody we know . . . is like that . . .'

'I say,' cried Martin suddenly, 'what about Fergusson. What was he doing round here tonight . . .'

'Major Fergusson, sir?' said Frost sharply. 'What was he doing 'ere, sir?'

'We met him on the way here,' said Gale.

'And he said we'd have our trouble for nothing if we were going to see Rigg,' said Martin, 'do you remember?'

''E said that, sir?'

'Yes, but he was referring to the fact that there was no light,' said Gale. 'He thought Rigg was out . . . '

'That's what he *said*,' said Martin.

'Fergusson's a strange chap,' said Evershed, 'always seems as if he had something on his mind . . . '

''E was very badly wounded . . . '

'Yes,' Evershed nodded, 'serious head injuries — but I don't think they would account for what I mean. It's a deep-seated worry of some kind.'

'I noticed the same thing,' said Simon Gale, 'when we met him on Sunday.'

'At one time,' said Doctor Evershed, 'I thought he was going to have a breakdown. He's been better lately . . . '

'Since the death of Hallam?' asked Gale.

Evershed frowned.

'It never struck me that way before, but — well, yes, you're right.'

'Quite a number of people seem relieved that Hallam's dead,' remarked Gale. 'You can sense it whenever his name is mentioned . . . Mrs. Langdon-Humphreys, Vanessa, Mrs. Barrett, Upcott . . . '

'Upcott — by Jupiter!' exclaimed

Martin excitedly. 'Doctor Evershed — you gave Upcott a prescription for barbitone this morning . . . '

'Did you, doctor?' asked Frost sharply, 'Yes — for insomnia . . . '

'Well, now,' said the Inspector, drawing a deep breath, 'that might be somethin' worth lookin' into . . . '

'Listen!' broke in Jill suddenly.

'What's the matter?' asked Simon Gale.

'There's somebody outside,' she said. 'I heard them . . . '

They listened. It was quite silent within the caravan, and in the silence they heard footsteps — hesitating footsteps on the rough ground outside.

'There *is* somebody out there,' whispered Gale. He moved cautiously nearer the closed door.

The footsteps came nearer, stopped, and then somebody began to mount the steps without.

'Who is it?' breathed Martin.

There was a gentle tapping on the door. After a moment it was repeated and a voice, a woman's voice, called softly:

'Rigg . . . are you there, Rigg?'

'It's Vanessa!' said Jill.

Simon Gale pulled the door open suddenly and Vanessa stared into the dimly lighted caravan in shocked and startled surprise.

'Oh . . . ' she said, 'oh . . . '

'Come in, Vanessa,' said Gale.

But she stayed, framed in the open doorway.

'I — I don't understand,' she said faintly, 'what are *you* all doing here? Where's Rigg . . . ?'

'Rigg's dead,' said Simon Gale, and then: 'Did you come to bring him a wreath, Miss Lane?'

7

I

Simon Gale paced up and down the long drawing-room at Easton Knoll. A pipe, that had long since gone out, was gripped between his teeth, and his sensitive fingers twisted and tugged at his beard. Jill, sitting uncomfortably on the edge of an easy chair, watched him and felt that any moment she would scream. At last her nerves would stand it no longer and she said irritably:

'For God's sake, Simon, stop prowling about like that!'

'I'm waiting to hear from Frost,' he grunted without pausing in his ceaseless perambulation.

'Can't you wait sitting down?' she said, desperately. 'You've been walking backwards and forwards for hours . . . '

'Hell's bells, what's the matter with you?' he demanded.

'Nothing,' she retorted, but there was an edge to her voice that belied her words. 'There's nothing the matter with me.'

He resumed his pacing, sucking on the empty pipe.

It was the morning following the discovery of the dead body of Rigg in the caravan — the Tuesday morning. Simon had been morose and silent for the rest of the Monday night and had said very little during the morning. For a little while longer Jill stuck it and then she said:

'Simon — how is it going to help Margaret if Rigg *was* poisoned with barbitone? Inspector Frost says himself it won't make any difference. They won't stop the execution. What are we going to *do*? This is Tuesday morning . . . '

'I know that, Jill.' Simon stopped and looked at her. 'Look here, you'd better get a grip on your nerves . . . '

'Oh, never mind my nerves!' snapped Jill crossly. 'There's so little *time* left and we're not getting anywhere. Why did Rigg have to die before he told us what he knew?'

'That was why . . . '

'And Margaret will die too . . . It's hopeless, Simon . . . Can't you see it's hopeless . . . ?'

'What's wrong with you this morning, Jill? You're all strung up . . . It's not hopeless . . . '

'I didn't think so until — we found Rigg.'

'You had high hopes of what he might have told us, hadn't you?' Gale nodded understandingly. 'So had I. It's the reaction that's making you feel like this . . . '

'I'm feeling all right, I tell you!' She broke out angrily.

'Stop being damned irritable!' bellowed Simon. 'You're not the only one this is affecting, you know? We're all feeling the strain . . . '

'I'm sorry, Simon,' she muttered.

'I know this sense of frustration is very nerve racking, but it's no good letting it get a hold of you . . . '

'Do you believe Vanessa's story?' Jill changed the subject abruptly. 'Why she came to Rigg's caravan last night?'

'I don't know,' he grunted.

'I don't believe it,' she declared. 'Is it likely Rigg would have sent her a note asking her to come? And do you suppose she *would* have come if he had — *Vanessa*?'

'It rather depends what was in the note, doesn't it? It said her aunt was in great danger . . . '

'That's what Vanessa told you,' said Jill suspiciously. 'There's no proof there ever was a note. She can't produce it . . . '

'She can't find it . . . '

'If there wasn't a note, she'd *have* to say that, wouldn't she?'

'Why do you think she came to the caravan, then?' he demanded.

'I think she came to make sure . . . '

'That the poison had worked — is that what you mean?'

'Yes.'

'You know what that implies?' said Gale, seriously.

'Well, why not?' she answered. 'Oh, I know Martin thinks she's wonderful — perhaps you do, too . . . but, it's got to be someone, hasn't it? How did Vanessa know that Doctor Wall teapot was in father's study . . . ?'

Before he could reply there was a tap on the door and Mrs. Barrett came in.

'Excuse me, Miss Jill,' she said. 'Major Fergusson's called. He wants to see Mr. Gale.'

'Oh, ask him to come in,' said Jill.

The housekeeper withdrew.

'I wonder what Fergusson wants?' muttered Gale.

'It must be something important,' said Jill. 'Major Fergusson doesn't usually pay social calls . . . '

'Sh — s — s,' warned Gale, as Mrs. Barrett ushered Major Fergusson into the room.

'I'm sorry to disturb you like this,' said Fergusson, 'but the matter is very important . . . '

'That's all right, Major Fergusson,' said Jill. 'Do sit down . . . '

'Thank you.' He hesitated, looking from one to the other.

'What did you wish to see me about?' prompted Gale.

Fergusson's confusion deepened. He

cleared his throat.

'Well, I wanted ... that is I'd rather ... ' he stopped, and then said hurriedly: 'Could I see you, alone, Mr. Gale?'

'Do you mind, Jill?' asked Simon.

'Of course not,' she got up, 'I've got to see Mrs. Barrett about lunch.'

'I hope you'll not think me rude, Miss Hallam,' said Fergusson apologetically, 'but the matter's rather a difficult one ... '

'There's no need to apologize,' said Jill. 'See you later, Simon ... '

When she had gone and the door was shut Gale said:

'Now, what is it, Major Fergusson?'

Fergusson fumbled nervously with his gloves.

'It's not very easy for me to — to speak of this, you understand, Mr. Gale?'

'Does it concern Hallam's death?' asked Simon.

'It may have a bearing on it indirectly. I don't know. You see, until you came here, it never occurred to me to doubt that Mrs. Hallam was guilty. There was no

145

reason to suppose that it could have been anyone else. But now there seems to be every reason for believing that Mrs. Hallam is innocent — particularly after the death of this man Rigg . . . '

'You've heard about that?'

'That's what made me make up my mind, Mr. Gale. However difficult and unpleasant it may be for me, I feel that it's my duty to acquaint you with the type of man Hallam was. It may help you a great deal. I cannot believe that my own case is an isolated one . . . '

'Your own case, Major Fergusson?'

'Aye . . . You would not think to look at me that I was a murderer, would you, Mr. Gale?'

Gale was startled. He had not expected this. Was Fergusson going to confess? The man's face was white and strained and dewed with sweat . . . He said:

'A murderer. Major Fergusson, do you realize what . . . '

'I did not kill Hallam, if that's what's in your mind,' said Fergusson. 'The murder I'm guilty of is worse than that.' He laughed bitterly. '*I* murdered nearly two thousand men — murdered them in cold blood . . . '

'I don't think I understand . . . '

Fergusson took out his handkerchief and wiped his forehead. His hands were shaking.

'It was during the war,' he said. 'I'll not go into details — even now I cannot think of it without a shuddering horror for what I did . . . '

'Major Fergusson, don't distress yourself . . . '

'I'm — I'm all right . . . It — it all comes back to me, you see — all the horror of it . . . '

'How did it happen?'

'I issued — the wrong order . . . the men were killed . . . '

'I see . . . '

'It was terrible . . . all those lives . . . '

'But, of course, it was a mistake . . . ?'

'The result was the same . . . Mistakes like that shouldn't be made. I shall never cease to blame myself for the death of those men . . . I don't want to say any more about that. I've told you enough for the purpose . . . '

'To offer you my sympathy seems a little futile . . . '

'I'd rather you didn't . . . it would do no good . . . '

'What has this to do with Hallam,' asked Gale.

'Hallam found out,' said Fergusson. 'You'll understand that only a few people — my superior officers and a handful of men who survived — knew what I did. Nobody round here knew. I was trying to forget — I couldn't, I don't think I ever shall — but I was trying. Hallam met one of the people concerned and they told him . . . ' Again he wiped his face. It was obviously causing him acute distress to talk about the tragedy that had ruined his life . . . After a pause he went on:

'Hallam sent for me one day and told me that he knew. After that he used to make me tell him exactly what happened . . . with all the details . . . over and over again until I felt I was going mad . . . '

'Hell's bells,' exclaimed Simon Gale. 'What a devilish thing to do . . . '

'He'd threatened to make the story public . . . he never did, but I was never sure when he *might* . . . . It was like a nightmare . . . '

'Yes — yes, I can understand . . . '

'It was such a relief when I heard he was dead — you can have no conception what a relief . . . '

'It must have been. He never attempted blackmail . . . ?'

'No, no — there was no question of that,' Fergusson got up and began to walk up and down. 'It was just for the *pleasure* it gave him . . . '

'There *are* people like that,' Gale spoke quietly and unemotionally. He wanted to calm this man's nerves which were raw and tortured. 'It's a mental kink. What makes you think that you weren't the only one to suffer from this unpleasant hobby of Hallam's?'

'Something he said to me once. He said: 'Nearly everybody's got something to hide, Fergusson. You'd be surprised how many of the people round here have . . . ''

'He never mentioned any — names?'

'No, he wouldn't do that. Once he'd given anybody's secret away, all the fun would have gone. It was taunting them with the possibility that he *might*, and watching them squirm, that amused him . . . '

'I guessed there was something like this, Major Fergusson, but I couldn't be sure. I'm very grateful to you for . . . '

'You've no need to be. Maybe I should have spoken before, but I couldn't see that any good purpose would be served. It's only that it may be of help to Mrs. Hallam that brought me here this morning. I've no desire, otherwise, to assist in finding the person who killed Hallam . . . '

'The murderer, in this case, deserves no mercy, Major Fergusson. He is quite prepared to let an innocent woman suffer for his crime unless we can prevent it . . . '

'Aye, I see that. Well, I hope you'll not have to divulge what I've told you . . . '

'I promise you it will go no further than ourselves, and possibly Inspector Frost. It may be necessary to tell him . . . '

'You must do as you see fit, Mr. Gale,

about that. You understand my position . . . ?'

'Yes. I don't want to sound interfering, Fergusson, but if you could only bring yourself to see this thing in its proper perspective . . . '

With a heralding tap the door opened and Mrs. Barrett came in.

'Doctor Evershed and Inspector Frost are here, sir,' she said. 'Shall I show them in?'

'Please, Mrs. Barrett,' said Gale.

Fergusson caught him by the arm as the housekeeper withdrew.

'I'd rather not meet them just now.' he said. 'Is there any . . . ?'

'Yes, go out by the window. There's a path that leads round to the drive . . . '

'Thanks. Goodbye . . . '

'Goodbye — and thank you,' said Gale.

He had barely gone before Frost and Evershed were shown in. They were followed by Jill.

'Can I come in now, Simon?' she asked. 'Oh, where's Major Fergusson?'

'He's gone,' said Gale. 'Well, what's the news, Inspector?'

'It was barbitone right enough, sir,' said Frost.

'Nearly a hundred and twenty grains — more than the lethal dose,' put in Evershed.

'Was it given him in the beer?'

'There were traces of barbitone in the dregs,' answered Frost. 'A considerable quantity . . . '

'That seems good enough,' grunted Gale. 'What about fingerprints?'

'There was only Rigg's on the bottle, sir.'

'That's conclusive — it was *murder* then,' said Gale.

'What do you mean?' asked Jill. 'How does that make it conclusive?'

'Hell's bells, don't you see?' he replied. 'The bottle must have been wiped *clean* before Rigg took hold of it. Otherwise there would have been the prints of the person who *sold* the beer to him . . . '

'That's a fact there would, sir,' said Frost, approvingly. 'Very smart of you to see that . . . '

'Rigg certainly wouldn't have bothered to wipe the bottle, so it must have been the person who planted it,' said Gale.

'Planted it?' repeated Jill.

'Yes, I think the beer was left in Rigg's caravan, ready primed with barbitone, while he was out. The murderer knew he wouldn't be able to resist it . . . '

'But surely Rigg would have wondered where it came from?' said Jill.

'Probably he did, but I doubt if it would have bothered him very much. He drank his gift from the gods and — that was the end.'

'It seems quite sound to me,' remarked Evershed.

'Yes, I'll say that was about the size of it, sir,' agreed Frost.

'All we've got to do now is find the person who give it 'im.'

'That's *all*,' said Gale sarcastically.

'Not so easy,' said Evershed.

'As a start,' suggested Simon, 'we might pay a visit to Robert Upcott . . . '

'Yes, I agree, sir.'

'It would be well worth finding out just *how* many of those barbitone tablets he has left,' said Gale.

8

I

Robert Upcott was surprised to see them, but he greeted them with his usual effusiveness.

'Why, this *is* a pleasant surprise,' he said. 'Delightful! Come in, *do* come in. Your arrival is really a blessing. Miss Ginch is in the drawing-room . . . '

'Good morning, sir,' said Inspector Frost, emerging from behind one of the pillars of the porch. Mr. Upcott looked startled and, Gale thought, a little frightened.

'Inspector Frost,' he said. 'Good gracious! I do hope you haven't come in an official capacity, Inspector?'

'Well, sir, partly,' answered Frost, 'an' that's a fact. Last night a man named Rigg . . . '

'Oh, yes, yes, what a dreadful thing, wasn't it?' Upcott shut the front door behind them.

'You know what happened, then?'

'Miss Ginch had just been telling me about it when you knocked. Shocking — positively shocking! It's really terrible the things one hears and reads about these days. Come into the drawing-room — I've just made some coffee . . . '

He ushered them into the dainty room, fussing round them in his usual irritating manner. Miss Ginch was perched on the extreme edge of a chair, and looking most uncomfortable.

'Miss Ginch,' cried Upcott, gaily, 'do you *see* who's called . . . '

'Good morning, Miss Ginch,' said Jill.

'Good morning, Miss Hallam. Good morning, Mr. Gale. Dear me, *and* Inspector Frost, too.' Miss Ginch's eyebrows rose in an arc. 'How very extraordinary.'

'Good mornin', miss,' said the Inspector.

'I called to collect some books that Mr. Upcott so *very* kindly promised for the sale — the jumble sale, you know,' said Miss Ginch, hastening to explain her presence, 'and he *insisted* that I should stay and partake of coffee . . . '

'You'd like coffee, Miss Hallam?' broke in Upcott. 'You'd *all* like coffee. You would — I'm sure you would . . . '

'Not for me,' answered Simon. 'Beer's more in my line . . . '

'Bottled beer?' said Mr. Upcott. 'I have some very excellent bottled beer. You would prefer beer, Inspector? I'm sure you would . . . '

'Well, I never say no to a drop o' beer, Mr. Upcott, an' that's a fact,' said Frost.

'I'll run along and get some at once,' said Upcott. 'Miss Ginch — would you mind pouring Miss Hallam out some coffee? There's a spare cup on the tray.'

He tripped away closing the door behind him. Miss Ginch picked up the coffee-pot.

'Is it true what I've heard,' she said, 'that that unfortunate man, Rigg, is dead?'

'It's true enough, miss,' said Frost.

'Evil livers come to evil ends. Yes, indeed,' said Miss Ginch as she poured out the coffee for Jill. 'I don't wish to be unchristian, but I cannot help thinking that the village will benefit.'

156

She nodded several times as she handed the cup to Jill.

'*Somebody* benefited, Miss Ginch,' said Simon Gale. 'Rigg was murdered.'

'Murdered?' Miss Ginch looked shocked. 'Dear me, how very terrible . . . I understood it was suicide . . . '

'He was poisoned — with barbitone. It was given to him in a bottle of beer . . . '

'Beer . . . ?'

The door opened and Mr. Upcott came in with a tray laden with bottles and glasses.

'Beer . . . ' repeated Miss Ginch, and eyed the tray thoughtfully.

'I'm sorry to have been so long,' said Upcott setting the tray down. 'I so seldom drink beer that I couldn't remember *where* I'd put it . . . '

Gale pointed to the tray.

'It was in a bottle of beer — just like one of those, Miss Ginch.'

'Dreadful — really dreadful,' said Miss Ginch, with a lady-like shudder.

'What are you talking about, Mr Gale?' asked Upcott in surprise. '*What* was in a bottle of beer?'

'The poison which killed Rigg,' said Gale.

'Mr. Gale says it *wasn't* suicide,' said Miss Ginch.

'Not *murder*?' exclaimed Upcott. 'Oh, no — that would be too shocking . . . '

'I'm afraid it *was* murder, Mr. Upcott, an' that's a fact,' said Frost, gravely. 'Rigg died from a large dose of barbitone . . . '

'Barbitone?' echoed Upcott in horror.

'Yes, sir. I understand,' the Inspector went on, 'that you 'ave in your possession a quantity of barbitone tablets which you got yesterday on a prescription issued by Doctor Evershed . . . ?'

'Good gracious, Inspector,' cried Upcott in alarm, 'you don't imagine . . . you can't be suggesting that I . . . ?'

'No, no, sir,' broke in Frost soothingly. 'I'm just checkin' up, that's all. 'Ave you still got those tablets, Mr. Upcott?'

'Yes, yes, of course. I took two last night — I have the remainder upstairs . . . '

'Could I see them, sir?'

'Really, Inspector, can't you take my word? I assure you . . . '

'I'm afraid I shall have to see them, sir,' insisted Frost.

'Oh . . . well . . . if you insist . . . I'll get them at once. Oh, dear, this is most upsetting . . . most upsetting . . . '

In a great state of agitation Upcott trotted from the room and they heard him climbing the stairs. Miss Ginch, her eyes shining with excitement, said with relish:

'Do you really suspect Mr. Upcott?'

'Not exactly, miss,' answered Frost stolidly, 'but, you see, barbitone *was* used an' we're tryin' to find where it came from . . . '

'Oh, dear me,' she said, almost wriggling with excitement, 'it's quite thrilling. Yes *indeed* — quite thrilling . . . '

'Do you really find it so, Miss Ginch?' asked Gale with interest. 'You're rather enjoying it, aren't you?'

'Oh, I wouldn't say that, Mr. Gale. The taking of human life is so very terrible . . . '

Upcott came back breathlessly.

'Here you are, Inspector,' he said,

holding out a round cardboard box. 'These are the tablets. There were fifty. I used two, as I told you — these are the remaining forty-eight. Count them — *do* count them . . . '

Frost peered into the little box.

'They look to be the right number, sir,' he said. 'I'll take these if you don't mind. Let you 'ave 'em back in a day or so . . . '

'Oh, you needn't bother,' said Upcott. 'Please keep them as long as you like. You're satisfied? I'm sure you're satisfied . . . ?'

'You've had quite a number of prescriptions for barbitone, haven't you, Upcott?' said Simon Gale.

'Yes, I've been taking them for a number of years,' said Upcott. 'They are really the only things that do my insomnia any good, you know . . . '

'Then those you have just given Inspector Frost could quite easily be old stock, couldn't they?' said Gale.

II

Inspector Frost gave a fat chuckle as they walked down the path after leaving the agitated Robert Upcott.

'You put the wind up him, sir, an' that's a fact,' he said.

'He *did* look a bit upset, didn't he?' said Gale.

'He nearly turned green,' said Jill. 'Do you really think he . . . ?'

'I don't know, Jill,' answered Gale. 'Everything we've got against him is only conjecture, isn't it?'

'You're right, there, sir,' agreed the Inspector. 'If he killed Rigg, then 'e must've killed Mr. 'Allam, an' what would 'e want to do that for? There's no motive . . . '

'There might be a very good motive,' said Simon. 'I learned something very interesting from Major Fergusson this morning . . . '

'What, sir?'

'I was going to ask you what he came for, Simon,' said Jill.

'I'll tell you both later,' said Gale. 'There isn't time now — we're nearly at

161

Mrs. Langdon-Humphreys' house, aren't we?'

'It's not very far . . . What's happened to Martin, this morning, Simon? I haven't seen him since breakfast . . . ?'

'I don't know — he went out somewhere,' answered Simon, 'I say, did you notice Miss Ginch? When she thought we suspected Upcott, I mean. She was almost licking her lips . . . '

'Yes, I saw,' said Jill. 'It was rather horrible . . . '

'She's a real nasty bit o' work, an' that's a fact,' said Frost.

'This will give her something to talk about,' said Jill, 'she'll spread it all over the village.'

'It's a bit 'ard on Mr. Upcott,' said the Inspector, ''specially if 'e 'adn't anything to do with it.' He chuckled again.

'What are you laughing at?' asked Jill.

'It's just occurred to me, miss,' he answered. 'We never 'ad that beer, did we?'

'Did you notice it was the same brand as that bottle at Rigg's place?' asked Gale.

The Inspector nodded.

'There's nothing much in *that*, sir,' he

162

answered. 'It's very common round these parts, that brand . . . 'Ere we are, this is Mrs. Langdon-Humphreys' house.'

They stopped in front of a small house standing on its own in about an acre and a half of ground. It was very trim and neat but Gale had expected something larger. He said so.

'She used to live at Pine Lodge,' said Jill. 'That's a lovely old place — bigger than Easton Knoll. She had to give it up when her husband died. She's not very well off now . . . '

'A tragedy that was,' said Frost, shaking his head. 'Thrown from 'is 'orse while 'e was 'untin' an' broke 'is neck.'

'When did that happen?' asked Gale.

'About three years ago,' said Jill.

'Has Vanessa always lived with Mrs. Langdon-Humphreys?'

'Oh, no,' she answered. 'She didn't come until after Mrs. Langdon-Humphreys moved from Pine Lodge. We'd never heard of her until then.'

It was Vanessa who opened the door to their ring.

'Oh . . . hello, Jill,' she said in surprise.

'Hello, Vanessa . . . can we come in?'

'Yes, of course . . . Martin's here . . . '

Jill's face changed. She looked annoyed.

'Oh,' she said, 'so *that's* where he went to?'

'Didn't you know?' said Vanessa. 'I thought that was why you'd come.'

'No, I didn't know,' said Jill, curtly.

Vanessa ushered them into the hall and shut the door.

'Come in here,' she said and led the way into the drawing-room. 'Auntie — here're Jill and Mr. Gale . . . '

'And Inspector Frost apparently,' remarked Mrs. Langdon-Humphreys, looking up from a piece of embroidery she was working on. 'Why have you come to see us, Inspector?'

'I'd like to ask Miss Lane one or two questions about last night, ma'am,' he said.

'Well, don't stand in the doorway,' said Mrs. Langdon-Humphreys. 'Come in and sit down.'

'Thank you, ma'am . . . '

'I didn't expect you'd all turn up *here*,' said Martin. 'I was just coming to look for you . . . '

'I'm sure you were, Martin,' said Jill. 'We wondered what had happened to you. I suppose we might have known . . . '

'Well, I thought — after last night — I'd just pop along and see how Vanessa was feeling,' he said.

'It was very nice of you,' said Vanessa.

'Yes, *very* sweet of you, Martin,' remarked Jill, acidly.

'What do you want to ask my niece?' demanded Mrs. Langdon-Humphreys, turning a cold stare on the Inspector.

Frost cleared his throat.

'Just one or two questions, ma'am,' he answered.

'My niece told you everything she could last night,' said Mrs. Langdon-Humphreys, carefully selecting a piece of silk from the basket beside her. 'I fail to see what else you can have to ask her?'

'I'm not quite clear on one thing, ma'am,' said Frost. 'It's about this note that Rigg's s'posed to have sent you, miss. Have you been able to find it?'

'No, I'm — I'm afraid I haven't,' answered Vanessa. 'I must have lost it . . . '

'Did you see it, Mrs. Langdon-Humphreys?' asked the Inspector.

'No — I knew nothing about it until afterwards. My niece was very foolish to take any notice of it . . . '

'It seems to me rather peculiar that she did,' said Gale.

'But I told you,' broke in Vanessa. 'It said that auntie was in danger . . . '

'And you wanted to find out what the danger was, is that it?'

'Yes — yes, that's it,' she answered eagerly.

'It seems quite a natural thing to do, Simon,' said Martin.

'It would be if Vanessa were anticipatory of any danger to her aunt,' said Gale. 'Were you, Vanessa?'

'Well — no, no, I wasn't,' she answered hesitantly, 'not until I got the note . . . '

'Then it seems extraordinary that you should go rushing off to see a man like Rigg, at that hour, just because he sends you a note,' said Gale. 'Did you know Rigg?'

'Only what I'd heard about him,' said Vanessa.

'My niece acted on a sudden impulse, Mr. Gale,' put in Mrs. Langdon-Humphreys, without looking up from her work. 'There's nothing extraordinary about it at all. Had she told *me* what she intended to do, I should have prevented it.'

'This note was delivered by 'and, I s'pose?' asked Frost.

'Yes ... I — I suppose so,' said Vanessa. 'I found it in the letter box ... '

'If it came by post there would have been a stamp on the envelope, miss ... '

'There may have been,' she answered, 'I — I don't remember ... '

'Well, there's no gettin' away from it — it's peculiar, an' that's a fact,' remarked Inspector Frost. 'It couldn't have come from Rigg, you know?'

'Why not?' asked Vanessa sharply.

'What do you mean, Inspector?' Mrs. Langdon-Humphreys looked up with sudden interest.

'Because you see,' said Inspector Frost, dropping his bombshell with deadly accuracy, 'Rigg couldn't either read or write ... '

9

I

It was quite evident that Inspector Frost's statement was unexpected. It produced a momentary, and rather weird, effect of suspended animation among his hearers. Vanessa was the first to recover.

'But that's impossible,' she declared, 'you *must* be wrong . . . '

'Are you sure of that?' asked Simon Gale.

'Oh, yes, sir,' said Frost. 'There's no doubt about it . . . '

'You never mentioned it last night,' said Martin.

'I didn't *know* last night,' said Frost. 'I was makin' some inquiries about Rigg this mornin' an' that fact came to light, sir. 'E couldn't even sign 'is own name.'

'But he must have been able to,' presisted Vanessa. 'The note he sent me was signed . . . '

'It's a great pity you haven't got it, isn't it, Vanessa?' remarked Jill.

'I don't know what happened to it,' said Vanessa. 'I've hunted everywhere. I thought I took it with me — when I went to the caravan . . .'

'Perhaps you dropped it on the way?' suggested Martin, helpfully.

'That's quite likely. Did you put it in your pocket?'

'I can't remember,' she answered, 'I may have — I was very worried and upset . . .'

'Well, it's a very funny thin', miss, an' that's a fact,' said the Inspector. 'I don't see how the note could have come from Rigg . . .'

'Are you insinuating that my niece is lying to you, Inspector?' said Mrs. Langdon-Humphreys, in a quiet but deadly tone.

'No ma'am,' he answered, 'but you must see that if this feller, Rigg, couldn't write, 'e couldn't have sent the note . . .'

'Perhaps he didn't,' said Simon Gale.

'If Vanessa says she received a communication from this man, Mr. Gale,' said

Mrs. Langdon-Humphreys, 'I see no reason to doubt that fact . . . '

'I wasn't suggesting that, Mrs. Langdon-Humphreys,' said Gale. 'I meant the note may not have come from Rigg . . . '

'But Vanessa says it was signed with Rigg's name,' said Jill.

'That doesn't necessarily mean that Rigg knew anything about it,' retorted Gale.

Inspector Frost looked interested.

'Do you mean, sir,' he asked, 'that somebody else . . . ?'

'Yes, somebody who thinks they are being very clever, Frost,' said Gale. 'They killed Hallam, and made it look as if his wife had done it. Now they've killed Rigg, don't you think it's possible they may be trying to involve Miss Lane?'

'Oh, but . . . ' began Vanessa.

'Be quiet, Vanessa,' snapped Mrs. Langdon-Humphreys.

'I see what you mean, sir,' said Frost. 'It's possible, I s'pose . . . '

'Well, quite obviously Rigg didn't write the note himself,' said Gale. 'He couldn't. He may have got someone else to write it for him, but I shouldn't think that was likely. The only other explanation is that it was written to bring Vanessa to the caravan . . . Was there any time mentioned in it?' He turned to Vanessa.

'Yes,' she said, quickly, 'After eight-thirty . . . '

'There you are, you see?' Gale went on. 'The writer intended to make sure that Rigg would be dead, and that we should be there, when you arrived on the scene . . . '

'It was a long time after eight-thirty before Vanessa *did* get there,' said Jill.

'I couldn't get away before . . . '

'She was waiting an opportunity of slipping out without my knowing, Jill,' said Mrs. Langdon-Humphreys. 'She imagined, quite rightly, that I should not have let her go.'

'Well,' said Frost, 'there may be somethin' in your idea, Mr. Gale — though, if the intention was to make us suspect Miss Lane, it was a bit of a hit-and-miss job. She might 'ave ignored the note altogether . . . '

'Ah!' said Simon Gale, looking directly

at Vanessa, 'that depends on what was in it . . .'

'What do you mean, Mr. Gale?' demanded Mrs. Langdon-Humphreys.

'I think you know very well what I mean,' he answered. 'What did the note *really* say?'

'I've told you,' said Vanessa.

'That's just what I don't think you have,' he remarked, quietly.

'Mr. Gale,' said Mrs. Langdon-Humphreys, acidly, 'I am loath to believe that you intend to be deliberately insulting . . .'

'You're quite right, I don't,' he interrupted. 'All I'm trying to get at is the truth . . .'

'I've no idea what you're talking about . . .'

'Let me put it this way,' he continued, 'what did Jonas Rigg know about you and Vanessa that you were so afraid he might make public?'

Vanessa uttered a low exclamation.

'I think,' said Mrs. Langdon-Humphreys, in her most majestic manner, 'that you must have taken leave

172

of your senses, Mr. Gale.'

'That's what was really referred to in the note, wasn't it?' he went on, ignoring this interruption. 'Not some hypothetical danger that you might be in?'

'No,' cried Vanessa, vehemently, 'no, no . . .'

'You thought Rigg had discovered the same thing that John Hallam had discovered,' said Gale, relentlessly. 'That's right, isn't it?'

'I refuse to listen to any more of this rubbish,' said Mrs. Langdon-Humphreys.

'Hell's bells,' exclaimed Simon Gale, angrily. 'Why don't you tell us the truth, both of you?'

'Simon . . . ' began Martin.

'Be quiet!' snapped his brother.

'How dare you speak to me like that, Mr. Gale,' said Mrs. Langdon-Humphreys.

'I'll tell you why I dare, Mrs. Langdon-Humphreys,' said Gale. 'Because at the present moment Margaret Hallam is under sentence of death for something she didn't do, and you are prepared to risk that sentence being carried out, sooner than suffer the slightest unpleasantness yourself . . . '

'It's not true,' cried Mrs. Langdon-Humphreys. 'It's not true . . . '

'It *is* true,' said Gale. 'I *know* the kind of man Hallam was. He liked to find things out about people, and hold his knowledge over their heads — it gave him a perverted pleasure to make them suffer. He knew something about *you*, Mrs. Langdon-Humphreys, which you're terrified may come out . . . '

'Absurd!' she declared. 'I never heard such nonsense . . . '

Gale swung round on Vanessa.

'Do *you* think it's nonsense?' he snapped.

She flinched.

'I . . . yes, yes, of course . . . of course I do,' she whispered. And then she suddenly burst into a flood of tears.

'Vanessa,' Martin came quickly to her, 'Vanessa, don't . . . '

'Go away,' she sobbed, 'go away . . . '

Mrs. Langdon-Humphreys rose to her feet.

'I think it would be better if you all went,' she said.

Gale shrugged his shoulders.

'Very well,' he said, coldly, 'but I should advise you to think over what I've said . . .'

'There is nothing to think over,' she said.

'If you *do* know anythin', ma'am,' put in Frost, 'that's likely to 'elp us, it's your duty to . . .'

'I am perfectly aware of my duty, Inspector Frost,' she said. 'I cannot see that it is part of it to allow my niece to be upset and myself insulted . . .'

'I'm sorry you should take that attitude, Mrs. Langdon-Humphreys,' said Gale.

'Simon is only trying to help Margaret,' said Jill.

'All and everything concerning John Hallam may be of help, Mrs. Langdon-Humphreys. Remember that after Thursday it will be too late — *nothing* will do any good then. How will you feel afterwards — knowing that you could have helped, and didn't . . .'

'Will you — please go?' Mrs. Langdon-Humphreys almost hissed the words.

'Yes, we'll go,' said Gale, 'but I don't envy either of you your thoughts . . . '

II

Inspector Frost lifted a white-capped tankard.

'Your very good health, Mr. Gale — your very good health, miss,' he said.

'Good luck,' said Gale.

'Cheerio!' said Jill.

They had dropped into the Hand and Flower after leaving Mrs. Langdon-Humphreys' house, because Simon Gale asserted that he must have lots of beer to wash away the nasty taste in his mouth.

'You know,' said Frost, wiping his lips, 'I thought you was carryin' things a bit high handed with those two, sir, but now you've told me about Major Fergusson, of course I can see what you was gettin' at. You think Mr. 'Allam was playin' the same game with 'er?'

'Yes — and with several other people as

well,' said Gale. 'Fergusson said he'd as good as admitted it . . . '

'I would never have believed that father could — could be so beastly,' said Jill.

'Queer form of amusement, but not so uncommon as you might think,' said Gale. 'Of course, Hallam carried it to unusual lengths — he was abnormal.'

'Well, you don't 'ave to look far for a motive for 'is murder, sir,' said Frost.

'So you're beginning to come round to my way of thinking, eh, Inspector?' asked Simon.

'I'm certainly beginnin' to believe that Mrs. 'Allam may not be guilty, after all, an' that's a fact, sir . . . '

'Oh, I'm so glad,' exclaimed Jill.

'But we've got a long way to go before we can say who is,' said Frost, shaking his head.

'At the moment it might be any one of them, mightn't it?' said Gale. 'Upcott, Mrs. Langdon-Humphreys, Vanessa, Miss Ginch, Fergusson . . . '

'Surely not Major Fergusson, Simon?' objected Jill. 'He wouldn't have come and told you about father if . . . '

'If he was clever he would,' broke in Gale, 'and our poisoner is very clever . . . '

'Clever enough to 'ave thought of sendin' that note to Miss Lane, sir,' remarked Frost.

Simon swirled the beer round in his tankard, and frowned at it.

'There's something about that I can't understand,' he said.

'What do you mean, sir?'

'*Was* there a note at all,' said Gale. 'If Vanessa had to find an excuse for coming to Rigg's caravan, that would have been as good a one as any, wouldn't it?'

'That would account for 'er not bein' able to find it . . . '

'There's another reason. If there *was* a note, and it contained some reference to this thing that both Vanessa and Mrs. Langdon-Humphreys are so anxious to hide — something that Hallam knew about them — they'd *still* pretend it was lost. I can't make up my mind which is the truth.'

'Whichever it is, you made 'em feel

proper uncomfortable, an' that's a fact, sir.'

'I meant to,' said Simon. 'I hope it may have some effect . . . '

'Martin was furious,' said Jill. 'That's why he went off in a temper . . . '

'I don't care a fig whether Martin's furious or not,' retorted Gale. 'There's only one important thing — and that's to get Maggie out of that condemned cell. We can straighten other things out afterwards.'

'An' we'll 'ave our work cut out to do it, an' that's a fact, sir,' said Frost. 'Two an' a half days — that's all we've got . . . '

'It's *got* to be time enough,' said Gale.

'Well, sir,' said Frost, 'I'll be able to 'elp officially now, since Rigg was murdered . . . '

'Yes, that's something to be thankful for,' answered Simon. 'We shall need all the help we can get . . . Jill, do you feel like throwing a little party this evening?'

She stared at him in astonishment.

'A party, Simon?'

'Yes — you might ask Upcott, Miss Ginch, Doctor Evershed — and you can try Vanessa and Mrs. Langdon-Humphreys if they'll come . . . oh, and Fergusson, too . . . '

'I'm sure Major Fergusson won't come,' she said. 'He never goes anywhere . . . '

'Perhaps you'd better leave him to me,' said Gale. 'I might be able to persuade him . . . '

'What's the idea?' asked Jill, curiously. 'Why do you want me to ask all these people to Easton Knoll?'

'Just a little experiment,' he replied.

She was going to question him further when the landlord came over.

'Oh, excuse me, Miss 'Allam,' he said confidentially, 'I forgot to mention it before. I 'ope there was no inconvenience caused over the beer . . . '

'The beer?' said Jill.

'Yes, miss,' answered the landlord. 'Yer see, I couldn't let your 'ousekeeper 'ave any bottled beer yesterday mornin' 'cos it 'adn't come in. I've got plenty now, if you should be wantin' any . . . ?'

'Oh . . . I see . . . thank you . . . ' she stammered.

'You'd better send a crate up to the house, landlord,' broke in Gale.

'Very good, sir. I'll 'ave it got up this afternoon.' The landlord nodded and went to attend to a new customer.

'Simon,' said Jill, a little bewildered. 'I don't understand . . . Mrs. Barrett evidently tried to get some bottled beer here yesterday morning . . . '

Inspector Frost pursed his lips.

'That's rather a rummy coincidence, sir, considerin',' he remarked.

'Yes, isn't it?' said Gale, thoughtfully. 'Very rummy . . . '

10

Jill stopped playing and got up from the piano as Martin came into the room. She had spent the afternoon alone. Simon Gale and his brother had both gone out immediately after lunch.

'Where's Simon?' she asked.

'I've no idea,' answered Martin curtly. He looked worried and ill-humoured.

'Where do you think he can have gone to?' asked Jill.

He shrugged his shoulders.

'Anywhere. Simon's a law unto himself. You'll realize that when you know him better . . . '

'I think he might have said where he was going.'

'Simon might do a lot of things that he doesn't,' grunted Simon's brother. 'There are times when he makes me sick . . . '

'I know — this morning was one of

them, wasn't it?' she said.

'Yes, it was . . . '

'You needn't snap *my* head off,' she retorted. 'It was nothing to do with me.'

'Vanessa was upset enough as it was,' he said, sulkily. 'Without Simon making it worse . . . '

'Don't you think Margaret's life is more important than upsetting Vanessa?' she said.

He took out a cigarette and lighted it.

'I wouldn't grumble if it was going to help Maggie — you ought to know that,' he said, inhaling deeply. 'But it won't. It's absurd to imagine that Vanessa had anything to do with your father's death . . . '

'Is it?' said Jill quietly.

'Of course it is,' said Martin. 'How could she? Can you imagine Vanessa poisoning anyone?'

'Do poisoners have some sort of outward and visible sign, then?' she asked.

'No — but Vanessa . . . Ridiculous!'

'What about Mrs. Langdon-Humphreys?' said Jill. 'Does she come under your championship too?'

'There's no reason why you should try and be funny about it,' he said crossly.

'I'm not . . . I don't think it's a little bit funny . . . '

'All I'm saying is that Simon might have shown more tact,' grumbled Martin. 'Vanessa had a pretty bad shock — coming to that beastly caravan and — and finding Rigg and all of us. It was only natural she should be upset. When everybody started in on her about that wretched note . . . '

'You must admit,' said Jill, 'that there's something very strange about that note . . . '

'I think Simon was right about it. It was obviously a trap to drag Vanessa into this thing . . . '

'Do you think so?'

'Of course it was . . . '

'I wonder . . . ?'

Martin flared up.

'Are you suggesting that there *wasn't* a note?' he demanded.

'It wouldn't be much good if I did, would it?' she snapped. 'If Vanessa *says* she had a note, she *must* have had a note . . . That's how you look at it, isn't it?'

'I believe her, if that's what you mean . . . ?'

'Oh, you'd believe her whatever she said,' she declared irritably.

'I don't know about that, but I'm sure she's telling the truth in this instance . . . '

'Well, I'm not!' said Jill.

Martin flung his half smoked cigarette into the fire. His face reddened and he looked very angry.

'I don't think you've any right to say that,' he exclaimed.

She looked at him and sighed suddenly.

'I wonder if you'd stick up for me like that?' she said.

'I suppose I would . . . yes, I'm sure I would.' The anger died out of his face. 'But you're different, Jill. You're much more capable of looking after your-self . . . '

'Am I?'

'Vanessa's so — so helpless . . . '

She laughed. It was a short and rather bitter laugh.

'You don't really know her very well, do you?' she said.

'What do you mean?'

'You don't know much about women, Martin . . . '

'Look here, I'm not exactly a school-boy,' he protested.

'Vanessa adopts that pose because it suits her,' said Jill. 'Can't you see that? It's useful, sometimes, to appear helpless and appealing. It gets you things that you *wouldn't* get otherwise . . . Vanessa's quite clever really . . . '

'You don't like her,' said Martin. 'That's why you say these things . . . '

'You're wrong, Martin,' she shook her head. 'I think she's a very nice girl, but she doesn't *fool* me. Underneath she's a little selfish and rather hard . . . '

'Well, I suppose most of us are,' he said.

'Yes — but when you say that Vanessa is 'helpless' . . . it's just silly . . . '

Mrs. Barrett came in and interrupted the argument — an interruption for which they were both thankful. The housekeeper wanted to know about the arrangements for that evening and when she had gone, Martin said:

'What's happening tonight, Jill? Who're coming?'

'Mr. Upcott, Doctor Evershed, Miss Ginch — I'm not sure about Major Fergusson — and Inspector Frost . . . '

'What's the idea?' he asked.

She shook her head.

'It's Simon's,' she said.

'What on earth's he up to now?' muttered Martin, frowning.

'I don't know, he didn't say,' said Jill. 'He asked me to invite those people for this evening, and I have, but I don't know what it's all about.'

'Didn't he want Vanessa and Mrs. Langdon-Humphreys?'

'Yes, I asked them both, but they didn't think they'd be able to come.'

Martin grunted.

'I'm not surprised after this morning,' he said. 'I wonder what Simon's playing at . . . ?'

'He said he wanted to try an experiment,' she said.

'And now he's vanished somewhere?'

'Yes.'

Martin thrust his hands into his pockets. His forehead wrinkled into a puckered frown.

'I wonder where the deuce he's gone to?' he muttered.

II

'In here, Hallam,' said the wardress, curtly.

Margaret Hallam walked slowly into the visitors' room, but her face lit up with pleasure when she saw who was awaiting her.

'Simon!' she exclaimed.

'Hello, Maggie,' he greeted with a grin. 'I thought it was time I popped in and had a look at you.'

'I'm so very glad to see you, Simon,' she said.

'How are you feeling?' He eyed her critically. 'You're not looking too bad, I must say . . . '

He took a step nearer and the wardress's voice broke in warningly:

'Keep the regulation distance from the prisoner, please.'

'All right, all right,' said Gale. 'I know. I've no files, hacksaws, bottles of arsenic, or other lethal weapons concealed about me . . . There you are, hands on the table according to the rules and regulations.'

He slapped his hands, palm downwards on the long table.

'The rules have to be obeyed,' said the wardress stolidly.

'They will be, my good woman,' he said. 'Don't worry . . . sit down, Maggie . . . '

She sat down and they faced each other across the dividing table.

'Have you come up from Easton Knoll?' she asked.

'Yes — I wanted to ask you one or two questions,' he said.

'Simon — have you found out anything?' she demanded, eagerly. 'Is there any chance . . . ?'

'Chance?' he replied. 'There's more than a chance. Don't worry — everything's going to be all right . . . '

She looked at him searchingly.

'Do you really mean that?' she said, 'or are you — just saying it to — to . . . ?'

'I mean it, Maggie,' he answered, gravely.

'What's happened?' she said. 'Tell me all about it — you must tell me, Simon . . . '

'I can't now, Maggie,' he said. 'I haven't got very long — and there's quite a lot I want to talk about . . . Did you know a man named Rigg?'

'Jonas Rigg?' she said. 'Yes, he's a poacher . . . '

'He *was* a poacher,' corrected Gale. 'He's dead — he was poisoned. Somebody put a large dose of barbitone in his beer . . . '

'Barbitone?'

'Yes. He was going to tell me something he saw on the night Hallam was killed. He was murdered before he had a chance . . . '

'But, Simon,' she exclaimed, excitedly, 'that means that I . . . if you tell the police they'll *have* to do something about me, surely? Doesn't it prove that I couldn't have . . . '

'No, it's not enough on its own,' he said. 'The police already know all about it, naturally. Inspector Frost is convinced, now, that there's been a mistake about you, and he's working with me to prove it. We'll have something definite soon . . . '

'It'll have to be very soon, Simon,' she said. 'If it's to do any good . . . '

'Don't worry about that, Maggie,' he said. 'Leave it to me. Now, listen . . . did you know that Hallam amused himself by finding out things about people — things they didn't want known — and held it over their heads? A sort of profitless blackmail?'

'No — did he do that?'

'Yes, there was no money about it — he did it purely for the pleasure of seeing them suffer . . . '

'I can imagine *that*,' she said. 'It would have appealed to John. He *liked* to see people suffer . . . '

'I'm sure that that was the motive behind his murder,' declared Gale. 'I think he stumbled on something really *serious* about somebody — something *criminal* — so that it was absolutely essential, for the safety of the person concerned, that he should die before he had a chance of revealing what he knew — the same as Rigg had to die for a similar reason . . . '

'But who . . . '

'That's the question — who?' Gale ran his fingers through his beard. 'I believe it was one of seven people — Robert Upcott, Mrs Langdon-Humphreys, Miss Ginch, Vanessa Lane, Major Fergusson, Doctor Evershed, or Mrs. Barrett . . . '

'Mrs. Barrett? Oh, no . . . that's absurd . . . '

'It's not so absurd as it sounds,' he replied. 'She had the best opportunity of anybody. Never mind that for the moment — you know all these people intimately, Maggie. Have you any idea at all — even the vaguest — what it was that Hallam could have found out about them? You needn't bother with Fergusson — I know what it was in his case . . . '

She shook her head.

'No, Simon. I'm afraid I can't help you . . . Oh! . . . '

'You've remembered something?' he said, quickly.

'No, I haven't . . . not really. I was just wondering if . . . '

'Go on, Maggie,' he urged as she paused. 'What?'

'Robert Upcott's wife — she . . . '

'Ran away with some man or other.'

'Oh, you know about that?' she said.

'Yes,' he answered, 'but what do *you* know about it?'

'Nothing . . . only nobody knew who it was . . . I wondered if there was something about *that* . . . John might have found out?'

'The whole thing was rather mysterious, wasn't it?' he asked.

'Yes . . . It could be that — with Upcott — couldn't it? I can't think of anything about any of the others . . . '

'Nothing concerning Mrs. Langdon-Humphreys or Vanessa Lane?' he persisted.

'Mrs. Langdon-Humphreys least of all,' answered Margaret. 'She always seemed to me rather formidable. I can't imagine there could be anything in *her* life that she'd be afraid of becoming known . . . '

'I'm quite sure there *is* something, all the same,' said Gale. 'Her husband broke his neck hunting, didn't he?'

'Yes, but it was all perfectly straightforward, Simon. There couldn't be anything in *that* . . . Vanessa's a different matter. I've always felt there was something strange about her . . . '

'How?' asked Gale sharply.

'I don't know,' Margaret looked troubled. 'It's difficult to put into words . . . It's just an impression . . . '

He nodded.

'I think I know what you mean,' he said, 'a sort of guardedness . . . as though she were afraid of giving something away?'

'Yes, partly, Simon. She's pretending all the time. She wants you to think she's one kind of person, while, in reality, she's something quite different . . . '

Simon Gale stared at her. Into his eyes came a queer expression — they seemed suddenly vacant and dead.

'Hell's bells,' he whispered softly. 'Hell's bells . . . '

'What's the matter, Simon?' asked Margaret.

'Maggie — do you remember that box of conjuring tricks my father gave me for a birthday present . . . ?' he asked.

'Simon,' said Margaret in bewilderment. 'What on earth . . . ?'

'It's all right, I'm quite sane,' he said. 'There was a book of instructions that we pored over together — remember?'

'Yes, but . . . '

'It said,' Gale went on rapidly. 'The secret of successful conjuring is the art of misdirection. You must make your audience think they've seen one thing, when actually they've seen something else. You pretend something is there when it isn't there at all . . . ?'

'Simon,' said Margaret, 'What *are* you talking about . . . ?'

'I believe that the same principles have been applied to the murder of John Hallam, Maggie — very successfully applied . . . '

Jill was in the drawing-room reading a magazine when Simon got back to Easton Knoll.

'Hello,' she said, as he came in. 'Where on earth have you been to?'

'I've been to see Maggie,' he said.

'Oh,' she said, throwing down the magazine. 'Is that where you went to? We were wondering, weren't we, Martin?'

Martin nodded. He was sprawling in an easy chair, staring at nothing.

'How is Margaret?' asked Jill.

'She's as well as you could expect in the circumstances,' said Simon. 'She sent her love to you, and asked me to thank you for your letter.'

'Poor Margaret,' said Jill.

'She's being very brave.' said Gale, 'but you can see the strain she's under . . . Fergusson's coming tonight. I've just seen him.'

'All of them are,' said Jill. 'Vanessa's just rung up to say that she and her aunt will come . . . '

'What's the idea, Simon?' asked

Martin. 'Why do you want all these people here tonight?'

'You'll see, Martin,' said Gale. 'What time are they coming, Jill?'

'Half-past nine.' She looked at the clock. 'They should be here any minute now.'

'And here's the first arrival,' said Martin, getting up.

They heard the knock on the front door and the footsteps of the housekeeper as she crossed the hall.

'I wish I knew what you were going to do, Simon . . . ' said Jill apprehensively.

'So do I,' muttered Martin . . .

'Miss Ginch,' announced Mrs. Barrett.

Miss Ginch came tripping into the room, her thin nose thrust forward and her small eyes darting inquisitively from one to the other.

'Come and sit over here by the fire, Miss Ginch,' said Jill. 'It's rather chilly this evening, isn't it?'

'Yes *indeed*,' said Miss Ginch. 'Such a *nasty* cold wind. I'm afraid my poor nose must be quite *blue* . . . '

'Not *quite*, Miss Ginch,' said Gale.

She looked at him suspiciously but his face was expressionless. There was another knock from the hall and they heard the front door opened.

'Here's somebody else,' said Martin.

'Dear me, are you expecting many people, Miss Hallam,' asked Miss Ginch. 'I'm so anxious to know why you asked *me* to come . . . '

'You'll know all in good time,' said Gale.

Mrs. Barrett ushered in Doctor Evershed, Robert Upcott, and Inspector Frost.

'We all met on the doorstep,' said Upcott. 'Quite a coincidence, isn't it? You know, I'm terribly intrigued to know why you've invited us here this evening, Miss Hallam. Tell me — *do* tell me?'

'I've just been asking the same thing, Mr. Upcott,' said Miss Ginch.

'You must ask Simon,' said Jill. 'He suggested it.'

'What's the idea, Gale?' asked Doctor Evershed.

'I'll tell you when the party's complete,' answered Simon.

'Do *you* know, Inspector Frost?' said Miss Ginch.

Frost shook his head.

'I know no more than you do, an' that's a fact . . . '

'Oh, dear,' said Miss Ginch, 'it all sounds *most* exciting.'

'I hope we shan't be kept too long in suspense,' said Upcott. 'I don't think I could bear it . . . '

'Who else are coming?' asked Evershed.

'Major Fergusson, Mrs. Langdon-Humphreys, and Vanessa,' said Jill.

'*And* Mrs. Barrett,' put in Gale, quietly.

'Mrs. Barrett?' Miss Ginch raised questioning eyebrows. 'Oh, do you mean the *housekeeper*? Really, I can't *think* what can be in your mind, Mr. Gale . . . '

'Perhaps that's just as well, Miss Ginch,' remarked Doctor Evershed pointedly.

'I'm sure I don't know what you mean by that remark, Doctor Evershed,' said Miss Ginch, her eyes sparkling angrily.

'Have you discovered anything further

about the death of that poor man, Rigg, Inspector?' inquired Upcott hastily. 'Such a dreadful thing — even though, of course, he was quite beyond the pale . . . quite, quite, beyond . . . '

'No, sir,' answered Frost, 'I'm afraid there's nothing definite as yet.'

'I do hope I'm no longer among your suspects,' said Upcott. He turned to Evershed. 'Do you know, Evershed, Inspector Frost *actually* thought that *I* might have used those tablets, you prepared for my insomnia, to kill Rigg. Incredible, isn't it? You agree — I'm sure you agree?'

'Oh, come now, Mr. Upcott,' protested Frost, 'that's not quite right, you know. I was only checkin' up in the normal course of routine, as you might say.'

'It must be very difficult, Inspector,' said Miss Ginch, 'to make *certain* about the source of these things — especially' — she shot a malignant glance at Evershed — 'in the case of *medical* men. It's so easy for *them* to obtain drugs of *any* kind . . . '

'The dangerous drugs have to be

accounted for, Miss Ginch,' said Evershed. 'A doctor has to keep records of such things . . . '

Mrs. Barrett appeared at the door.

'Major Fergusson,' she announced.

Fergusson came in quickly. He gave a sharp look round, nodded in a general greeting, and went over to Jill.

'Good evening, Major Fergusson,' she said. 'I'm so glad you were able to come. I think you know everybody, don't you?'

'Pretty well everybody,' he said.

''Evening, Fergusson,' said Evershed.

'So *unusual*, Major Fergusson, to see you at any of our little functions,' said Miss Ginch.

'But how *sensible*,' remarked Upcott. 'They're nearly all so appallingly boring . . . '

'Come over here, Fergusson,' said Gale.

'Shall I bring the coffee and sandwiches now, Miss Jill?' asked Mrs. Barrett.

'I think we'll wait for Mrs. Langdon-Hum . . . ' began Jill, and broke off as there came a knocking on the door.

'They're here now,' said Martin. 'I'll go, Mrs. Barrett . . . '

He hurried out of the room. Jill looked after him and gave a little twitch to her shoulders.

'Now we shall know what we're *all* here for, shan't we?' said Upcott. 'I must confess I'm feeling terribly curious . . . '

Mrs. Landon-Humphreys sailed into the room majestically. Vanessa followed rather nervously with Martin.

'I'm afraid we're rather late, Jill,' said Mrs. Langdon-Humphreys. 'We didn't make up our minds to come at all until almost the last minute, as you know . . . '

'You're not very late,' said Jill. 'Major Fergusson's only just arrived . . . '

'Sit over here, Vanessa,' said Martin, dragging forward a chair. 'Here's a chair for you, Mrs Langdon-Humphreys . . . '

'Thank you.' Mrs. Langdon-Humphreys sat down and looked about her. 'I can't imagine why you've asked us here this evening, Jill,' she said.

'Yes indeed,' said Miss Ginch. 'We're all wondering *that*, Mrs. Langdon-Humphreys. I understand it was Mr. Gale's idea . . . '

'Oh, was it?' Mrs. Langdon-Humphreys' face hardened.

'Now that everyone's here,' said Simon Gale, walking over to the fireplace and facing them, 'there's no reason why your curiosity shouldn't be satisfied . . . Put down that tray, Mrs Barrett, and please don't go. This concerns *you* just as much as anybody else.'

The housekeeper, who had come in with a tray of coffee and sandwiches looked at Jill.

'You wish me to stop, Miss Jill?' she asked.

'You heard what Mr. Gale said,' said Jill.

Mrs. Barrett set the tray down and quietly effaced herself behind her mistress.

'I asked Jill to invite you all here this evening for a special purpose,' said Gale. 'You know the reason I came here in the first instance? To find out the truth about the murder of John Hallam. The case against Mrs. Hallam was so strong, and appeared so obvious, that the police did not consider it necessary to carry their inquiries any further. That's right, isn't it, Inspector?'

'Yes, sir, I'm afraid it is,' agreed Frost. 'You can't altogether blame us . . . '

'I'm not,' said Gale. 'I'm just stating a fact. But I was certain that Maggie hadn't poisoned her husband. I've known her since childhood, and I know that she is absolutely incapable of killing anyone *that* way. If Hallam had been stabbed, or shot, anything but poisoned, I could have believed that she might have done it. But the poisoner's mentality is of a special kind, and it's not Maggie's. There's nothing underhand or secretive in her character . . . '

'How very fond of Mrs. Hallam you must be, Mr. Gale,' said Miss Ginch, with unmistakable innuendo in her tone.

'It's not a question of *fondness*, Miss Ginch,' retorted Gale. 'It's a question of *knowing* a person . . . '

'All that may be true,' broke in Mrs. Langdon-Humphreys, 'but I cannot see why you asked us here this evening to tell us . . . '

'It was not for that,' said Gale. 'I asked

you here — all of you — to make an appeal . . . '

'I don't quite understand . . . ' said Evershed. 'An appeal . . . ?'

'Yes,' said Simon Gale. 'Each one of you is hiding something . . . '

There were murmurs of protest.

'Oh, yes, you are,' he went on. 'John Hallam knew something about each one of you which you are trying to conceal . . . '

'In my case you're absolutely wrong,' bleated Upcott. 'Absolutely . . . '

'I thought we had gone into all that this morning?' said Mrs. Langdon-Humphreys, acidly.

'You're quite right,' agreed Gale, 'but we didn't go into it far enough! There's no time for consideration of people's feelings. This is Tuesday evening — on Friday morning Margaret Hallam will be hanged by the neck until she is dead . . . '

'Oh!' It was Miss Ginch who uttered the cry.

'It's not very pleasant to remember that, is it?' said Gale, looking from one to the other. 'But it will happen unless we can find out the truth in time . . . '

'But, my dear sir,' said Upcott, 'how can *we* help?'

'By every one of you telling the truth,' answered Gale. 'What *was* it that Hallam knew about each individual one of you that you are so frightened might become known?'

'So far as *I* am concerned,' said Miss Ginch, with conscious rectitude, 'I've nothing whatever to conceal.'

'Neither have I,' asserted Upcott.

'Are you including me in this?' asked Doctor Evershed.

'I'm including all of you,' said Simon Gale.

'It's fantastic — quite fantastic,' declared Upcott.

'Yes *indeed*,' agreed Miss Ginch. 'It might apply to *others* but certainly not to *me*. My life is quite open . . . '

'Absolute nonsense!' said Mrs. Langdon-Humphreys, angrily. 'Had I known that *this* was what you wanted to see us about, Mr. Gale, I should not have come . . . '

'I think you should heed what Mr. Gale

has said — all of you.' It was Major Fergusson who spoke. 'If by withholding anything you know, Mrs. Hallam has to suffer, it would be a terrible tragedy . . . '

'I cannot see how this concerns *you*, Major Fergusson,' said Mrs. Langdon-Humphreys.

'It concerns me to this extent,' answered Fergusson, and his face had gone a shade whiter and there was a strained look about his eyes. 'Hallam found out something about *me*, and made my life a hell . . . '

'Good for you, Fergusson,' muttered Simon Gale.

Miss Ginch's eyes glistened.

'Dear me, how interesting,' she said. 'Whatever was it, Major Fergusson?'

'I don't think it's necessary that you should be told that, Miss Ginch,' said Fergusson quietly, but in a tone that sent the red into her thin cheeks. 'I have told Mr. Gale, and that's all that matters.'

There was a pause — an uneasy silence.

'Well, what about the rest of you?' said Gale. 'Are you going to follow Major

Fergusson's example?'

Still silence. Somebody cleared their throat.

'Understand this,' he went on. 'I *mean* to know, and I *shall* know — even though the knowledge may be too late . . . '

'Too late!' It was like an echo and it came from Vanessa.

Mrs. Langdon-Humphreys rose to her feet.

'I'm afraid we shall have to be going, Jill,' she said, curtly.

'No,' said Vanessa, suddenly. 'No, I'm not going . . . '

'What do you mean, Vanessa?' demanded Mrs. Langdon-Humphreys.

'I'm not going,' said the girl defiantly. 'Mr. Gale, there's something I want to tell you . . . '

'Vanessa!' said Mrs. Langdon-Humphreys, warningly.

'It's no good, auntie, I can't . . . ' There was a dangerous edge to her voice.

'Vanessa . . . will you be quiet . . . ?'

'No, no, no . . . ' Vanessa's voice rose, shrilly, hysterically. 'I won't be quiet any longer. I'm going to tell them the truth . . . '

11

I

'Vanessa, I'm ashamed of you,' said Mrs. Langdon-Humphreys, sternly, as the girl broke into a fit of uncontrollable sobs. 'Stop that crying immediately and behave yourself . . . '

'Please don't interfere,' said Gale.

'I shall certainly interfere,' snapped Mrs. Langdon-Humphreys. 'My niece is overwrought and hysterical. She doesn't know what she's saying . . . '

'I do,' said Vanessa, through her sobs.

'Vanessa . . . ' said Martin, soothingly.

'Come along, Vanessa, I'm going to take you home,' broke in Mrs. Langdon-Humphreys.

'Well, really,' said Miss Ginch. 'If Miss Lane *has* anything to say, I *do* think she should be allowed to do so . . . '

'I've no doubt you do, Miss Ginch,'

said Mrs. Langdon-Humphreys, sarcastically, 'in the hope that it would provide you with a tit-bit of scandal to retail . . . '

'I consider that remark *most* insulting,' said Miss Ginch. 'I . . . '

'Jill,' interrupted Gale, 'take Vanessa into the study. She can tell me anything she wants to in private . . . '

'All right, Simon . . . '

'Mr. Gale,' said Mrs. Langdon-Humphreys, 'I insist . . . '

'You will stay in here with the others,' said Gale, curtly.

'I shall do nothing of the kind . . . '

'Oh, be quiet!' said Vanessa, recovering a little. 'I'm going to tell them and nothing will stop me . . . '

'Doctor Evershed' — Mrs. Langdon-Humphreys appealed to him — 'you can see that my niece is not in a fit state to . . . '

'It's useless appealing to me,' he replied shortly.

'I'm perfectly all right,' said Vanessa, dabbing at her eyes with Martin's handkerchief.

'We'll go into the other room, Vanessa,' said Gale. 'Come on, Jill . . . '

He opened the door for them.

'Vanessa — Vanessa, listen . . . '

Mrs. Langdon-Humphreys' voice was cut off abruptly as Gale shut the door.

'Whatever you tell me need go no further, Vanessa,' he said as they crossed the hall. 'Unless it's absolutely necessary . . . '

'I've been . . . so worried . . . wondering what I ought to do,' she said.

Jill opened the study door and switched on the light.

'You're shaking, Vanessa,' she said, when they had entered the room and closed the door. 'Sit down here . . . '

The girl shrank back.

'No — no, I won't sit *there*,' she cried. 'That's where — he sat . . . '

'Do you mean — Hallam?' asked Gale. She nodded.

'But I never knew you'd been in here before,' said Jill. 'When did you come?'

'It was — quite a long time ago,' said Vanessa. 'After he told us that he — knew . . . '

'What did he know, Vanessa?' asked Gale.

'I don't know how he found out, but he did,' she replied in a voice that shook a little, 'and — and he was *beastly* about it . . . to both of us . . . I thought, when he died . . . nobody would ever know — and then I got that letter from Rigg . . . and *he* knew too . . . '

The door was thrown open and Mrs. Langdon-Humphreys burst into the room.

'Vanessa,' she exclaimed agitatedly. 'You haven't said anything? You haven't told them . . . ?'

'Mrs. Langdon-Humphreys,' snapped Gale, angrily, 'will you let your niece . . . '

'That's it,' cried Vanessa, 'that's what everyone thinks, but it isn't true . . . '

'Vanessa . . . '

'I'm not her niece,' Vanessa went on rapidly. 'Oh, don't you understand . . . ? She's not my aunt as we've always pretended. She's my mother . . . '

II

It was a quarter to nine on the following morning when Inspector Frost was shown into the drawing-room. Simon Gale was alone — pacing up and down and smoking furiously.

'Good morning, Mr. Gale,' said Frost. 'I hope I'm not too early for you . . . '

'No, I had breakfast an hour ago,' answered Gale. 'Sit down.'

'Thank you, sir.' The Inspector pulled forward a chair. 'Well, your little party last night wasn't altogether a waste of time, an' that's a fact . . . '

'A ha'porth of bread to an intolerable deal of sack . . . ' said Gale.

'Eh?' Frost looked slightly bewildered.

'Rather an apt quotation — Shakespeare,' said Gale.

'Oh, I see, sir. You know I'd never have thought anything like that about Mrs. Langdon-Humphreys. Flabbergasted me, it did, when you told me . . . '

'It's not a very new thing,' grunted Gale. 'A marriage arranged by the family

213

— a brief romance, and the consequences. Lane died two years after Vanessa was born. His sister looked after the child until that hunting accident to Langdon-Humphreys made it possible for Mrs. Langdon-Humphreys to have her daughter with her . . . '

'It's understandable why she was so anxious it shouldn't come out,' said Frost. 'There'd 'ave been a first-class scandal in a place like this, an' that's a fact . . . '

'Yes . . . a pretty strong motive, that, Inspector,' said Gale.

'That's what I've been thinkin', sir.'

'But we've got to remember the letter — the one that was supposed to have come from Rigg,' said Gale. 'Vanessa didn't lose it. She couldn't show it before because it mentioned her real relationship to Mrs. Langdon-Humphreys. But I've got it now. Here it is.' He took a letter from his pocket and held it out to Frost. 'You see it's printed in capitals with a pencil — mis-spelt and illiterate — just as Rigg might have written it . . . '

'But didn't, sir . . . H'm, yes . . . I see . . . '

'That's just the point, Inspector. Rigg *didn't* write this — we know that, because he *couldn't* write. But *somebody* wrote it, knowing that it would bring Vanessa to the caravan that night — and the person who wrote it knew what Hallam knew — that Vanessa was Mrs. Langdon-Humphreys' daughter . . . '

'Unless Mrs. Langdon-Humphreys, or Miss Lane wrote it themselves, sir.'

'Yes, that could be. You mean to provide an excuse for Vanessa coming to the caravan? She had to think up something quickly when she found us there to account for her presence . . . ?'

'Yes.'

'If that's the case, it can only mean one thing,' said Gale gravely.

'That one or other of 'em murdered Mr. 'Allam an' Rigg, sir.'

'Yes . . . but if they did why hand us the motive on a plate? Vanessa *needn't* have said anything last night . . . '

'You're right there, sir,' agreed Frost. 'I

wonder if 'Allam knew anything about anybody else?'

'I'm quite sure there was something he'd found out about Upcott,' said Gale. 'It's obvious from the man's whole manner . . . '

'An' he's not givin' anything away,' declared Frost with conviction. 'You won't find 'im comin' forward an' tellin' you what it was.'

'Or Miss Ginch, either,' said Gale.

'Do you think she was another one, sir?'

'Yes, I do. She was much too eager to insist that nobody could know anything to *her* detriment . . . '

'Well,' said Frost shaking his head, 'It's a proper mix up, an' that's a fact. An' we 'aven't much time to straighten it out. Today's Wednesday, sir. We've got to find the right person, an' prove they did it, before tomorrow night — if it's goin' to do Mrs. 'Allam any good . . . '

'I think we shall,' said Simon Gale. 'I'm beginning to get a glimpse of the pattern behind it all. It's very hazy, but it's coming clear.'

'What is, sir?'

'A portrait of the murderer, Frost,' answered Gale, seriously. 'Not the portrait of a face, but the portrait of a *mind* — a mind that thinks and acts in a certain definite way . . . '

'You're gettin' a little beyond me, there, sir,' said the Inspector.

'Don't you see? When you know what the *mind* of the murderer is *really* like,' said Gale. 'You've got a *personality*, and it won't be difficult to fit that personality with a face — and a *name* . . . '

III

'If you're going to call on Doctor Evershed, Simon,' said Jill, two hours later, as they walked down the High Street, 'I'd better meet you afterwards. I must go into the grocer's and order some things for the house . . . '

'All right,' he said. 'Meet me in the pub. I don't expect I'll be very long . . . '

'I suppose Martin has gone chasing after Vanessa again?' she said.

217

'Not this time, he hasn't,' said Gale. 'He's doing a little job for me . . . Hell's bells! Here's the Ginch woman . . . '

Miss Ginch had spotted them from the other side of the road and, altering her course, came tripping over.

'I'm just going in here,' said Jill, hurriedly. 'You can have her all to yourself, Simon.'

She dived into a shop.

'Good morning, Mr. Gale,' said Miss Ginch, 'isn't it *lucky* that I should run into you like this . . . ?'

'Is it, Miss Ginch?' said Simon, without any marked degree of enthusiasm.

'Yes, indeed. I was on my way to Easton Knoll to see you . . . '

'What about?' he asked.

'I was so *impressed* by what you said last night, Mr. Gale,' she said, 'I felt I just *had* to tell you . . . '

'So Hallam *did* know something about you, Miss Ginch?' he said.

She looked shocked.

'Oh, no — not about *me*,' she answered, hastily. 'What I wanted to tell you is about Doctor Evershed . . . '

'Oh, I see,' said Gale.

'Of course,' said Miss Ginch rapidly. 'I wouldn't *dream* of saying anything if you hadn't pointed out how important it is that everyone should tell what they know . . .'

'And what do you know about Doctor Evershed?' he asked.

Miss Ginch looked quickly up and down the street and leaned towards him.

'Only that there *was* something that poor Mr. Hallam knew about him,' she said, confidentially. 'I've no doubt that Doctor Evershed will deny it, but I *know* there was . . .'

'How do you know?'

'You must promise that you won't mention *me* in the matter, Mr. Gale,' she said. 'People are *so* peculiar, you know. They always credit you with entirely the wrong motive . . .'

'Most unfortunate, Miss Ginch, isn't it?' he said. 'What did Hallam know about Doctor Evershed?'

'Well, I don't really know *what* it was,' she confessed. 'But there was something. Yes indeed. You see, I overheard them

219

quarrelling one night . . . '

'When?' he demanded.

'It was a few weeks before Mr. Hallam was killed,' said Miss Ginch, warming to her story. 'I was on my way home from the Vicarage — the choir boys' outing, I think it was — yes, that was it, or was it the Christian Mothers' Guild? I'm not quite sure . . . '

'Does it matter?' said Gale impatiently.

'Well, no — not *really*. But I like to be accurate in all things . . . '

'The important thing is what happened,' said Gale.

'Well, there's a short cut from the Vicarage to my little cottage,' Miss Ginch went on, 'a lane that skirts the grounds of Easton Knoll. Very few people use it, and I was *most* surprised to hear voices, just beyond a sharp bend in the lane. I want you to understand that I had no intention of eavesdropping, Mr. Gale . . . '

'No, no, of course — that's the last thing you would do, Miss Ginch . . . '

'They were *men's* voices, you see, and it's a very *lonely* place. I was a woman and you hear of such *dreadful* things, don't you? I hid in the hedge, hoping that they would go away, and then I recognized the voices — they belonged to Doctor Evershed and Mr. Hallam.'

She paused to see what impression this information had made, but Gale's face was expressionless.

'Go on, Miss Ginch,' he said.

'I was afraid to venture too near, so I couldn't hear *all* that was said, but I did hear Doctor Evershed say: 'Unless you keep quiet, I won't answer for the consequences.' I don't know what Mr. Hallam replied to this, his voice was too low, but Doctor Evershed answered: 'You can do as you please, but, remember, I've warned you . . . ''

'What happened then?' asked Gale.

'They both walked away, and I couldn't hear anymore,' Miss Ginch sounded disappointed. 'But they were both very angry. I could tell by the tone of their voices . . . '

'It's very kind of you to have passed this information on to me,' said Gale.

'I felt that it was my duty,' said Miss Ginch, virtuously. 'I did so *agree* with all

221

you said last night. I can only hope that my poor contribution will be helpful. I never *imagined*, of course, that what I heard could be of any *consequence*, until you said . . . '

'Naturally, Miss Ginch,' Simon tried to keep the disgust he felt out of his voice.

'I should have spoken last night,' she said, 'only you were so *occupied* with Miss Lane. I cannot conceive what she could possibly have to tell you . . . '

'I'm quite sure you'd never guess, Miss Ginch,' he said.

'Of course,' said Miss Ginch, in eager invitation, 'I would never *dream* of repeating anything you *told* me in confidence, Mr. Gale . . . '

'Can I absolutely *rely* on that, Miss Ginch?' asked Simon.

'Yes — yes indeed,' she declared, almost licking her lips in expectation.

'I'm so glad,' he answered. 'It's always a help to know there is *someone* who is absolutely reliable, Miss Ginch. Good morning.'

He nodded and walked quickly away leaving her standing staring after him in furious disappointment.

'Oh!' she muttered to herself, 'Oh! Well, really . . . *really* . . . '

IV

Doctor Evershed came to the door himself in answer to Gale's ring.

'Oh, hello,' he said. 'Come in . . . '

He led the way into his surgery and indicated a chair.

'Sit down,' he said. 'Cigarette?'

'No, thanks,' said Gale. 'I always smoke a pipe . . . '

'Carry on then,' said Evershed. He took a cigarette from a box and lit it. 'What did you wish to see me about?'

'Fergusson,' answered Gale, stuffing tobacco into his pipe.

'What about Fergusson?'

'He's been one of your patients for some time, hasn't he?'

'Yes.'

'I know this is all wrong,' said Simon, 'doctors are not supposed to talk about their patients — but in view of the circumstances, I'm hoping you'll stretch a point . . . '

'That depends on what you want to know,' said Evershed.

'What are the general effects of those head wounds?'

'Oh, I see,' Evershed nodded. 'H'm . . . well, I can't see why I shouldn't tell you that. I take it you don't want the medical terms . . . ?'

'No, I don't suppose I should understand them . . . '

'Well, the main symptom is intermittent headaches — pretty violent while they last.'

'And — what else?' said Gale.

Evershed gave him a sharp glance.

'Look here,' he said. 'What's at the back of your mind?'

Simon struck a match and began to light his pipe.

'Would there,' he said between puffs, 'be — lapses? Periods when Fergusson was not quite sure what he was doing — or had done?'

'Thought that was what you were getting at . . . '

'Well?'

'There *could* be,' said Evershed, thoughtfully.

'Has such a thing happened to Fergusson — to your knowledge?'

'No . . . no, I don't know of any instance of the kind . . . '

'But it's possible? He might do something that he wouldn't remember anything about — afterwards?'

'Yes, that could happen.' Evershed stubbed out his cigarette. 'Are you suggesting that Fergusson murdered Hallam during a mental blackout, and doesn't *know* he's done it?'

'I'm just wondering if it's possible . . . ?'

'Oh, it's possible enough. But — I doubt it. He'd have had to have had *another* mental blackout to kill Rigg, wouldn't he?'

'You think it's far-fetched?'

'Yes. It's absurd . . . '

'But — if he was subject to these — lapses — wouldn't any sudden excitement, or strong emotional upheaval, be likely to bring one on?'

'That's true. Candidly though, I think you're on the wrong track . . . '

'I'm not on any track, Evershed,' said Gale. 'I'm just shunting about until I find one. By the way, did *you* ever threaten Hallam?'

'*Threaten* Hallam?' Evershed shook his head. 'Good lord, no!'

'Are you — quite sure of that?'

'Of course I'm sure — why should I threaten Hallam?'

'I don't know — I was hoping you might tell me . . . '

'Out with it, Gale,' said Evershed, curtly. 'What's the idea . . . ?'

'You were overheard quarrelling with Hallam . . . '

'Nonsense,' said Evershed, testily. 'I never quarrelled with Hallam in my life. Don't know what the devil you're talking about. Who said so?'

'It was in a lane — near Easton Knoll,' said Simon Gale. 'You're supposed to have said to Hallam: 'Unless you keep quiet, I won't answer for the consequences.' It was a few weeks before the murder . . . '

'I never,' began Evershed, and then he suddenly burst out laughing. He laughed until the tears ran down his cheeks. 'Excuse me Gale, but it's really funny.' He wiped his eyes. 'I remember now. I wasn't *threatening* Hallam. I was *prescribing* for him. He'd been out of sorts, running a slight temperature, nothing serious, but there was an epidemic of influenza about. He wouldn't do what I told him, stay indoors and rest. I met him out that evening, and told him just what I thought about it. We both got a bit angry . . . '

'That's the explanation, is it?'

'Yes. Satisfied?'

'It's a very good explanation,' said Gale. 'If it wasn't true, I should be able to congratulate you on your ingenuity . . . '

'But since it is, you can't. What a pity . . . '

'Isn't it?' said Gale. 'Ingenuity is so much rarer than truth . . . '

'In this village,' said Evershed, 'it takes a great deal of the first to discover even a tiny particle of the latter . . . '

'Yes . . . yes,' said Gale, thoughtfully, 'I don't think you realize just how right you are . . . '

V

'Some more tea, Simon?' asked Jill.

'No, thanks,' he shook his head.

It was nearly half-past four and they were having tea in the drawing-room at Easton Knoll.

'Some more cake?' she asked.

'No thanks.'

She nibbled on a biscuit.

'What time is Martin likely to be back, Simon?'

'It all depends how long it takes him to finish his business,' said Gale.

'Where's he gone?'

'Up to town. There are one or two things I want from the studio . . . '

'Is he going to see Margaret?'

'He may do — if there's time . . . '

She poured herself out another cup of tea.

'Do you think you will be able to . . . to

save her?' she asked.

'If things work out as I hope they will — yes . . . '

'Have you any idea who it was?'

'Well . . . ' he pursed his lips.

'Simon, you *have* . . . '

'It's only the very vaguest notion, Jill . . . '

She leaned forward eagerly.

'Who, Simon? Tell me who . . . ?'

He shook his head.

'Not now,' he said. 'I've got to think it all out . . . I'll tell you tomorrow . . . '

'Tomorrow,' she said, and her face clouded. 'That's the *last* day, Simon.'

'Yes . . . ' he said. 'Yes, I've *got* to be right. There'll be no time to rectify a mistake . . . '

'If you're wrong . . . Simon, you *mustn't* be wrong. I couldn't go on living here without Margaret . . . '

'What would you do?' He got up and leaned on the mantelpiece, looking down at her.

'Sell the house, I suppose,' she said, 'or shut it up and go and live in London. I couldn't stay here — in this huge house

— all on my own.'

'You ought to get married, Jill,' he said.

She dropped her eyes.

'I don't think — that's very likely,' she said.

'I shouldn't let Vanessa worry you too much,' said Simon Gale meaningly.

She looked up quickly. He met her gaze with a quizzical smile.

'Vanessa? What do you mean, Simon?' she asked.

'Don't pretend, Jill,' he said. 'I know how you feel about Martin . . . '

'Oh . . . ' she breathed.

'It's very obvious, you know . . . '

'I didn't mean it to be,' she said, in a low voice.

'Never mind — things will sort themselves out,' he said. 'Vanessa won't worry you in the future . . . '

That startled her.

'Simon,' she exclaimed. 'You don't — you don't mean . . . ?'

The door opened and Mrs. Barrett came in.

'Miss Jill, that girl, Agnes Potter, wants to see you . . . '

'Agnes Potter?'

'Mrs. Potter's daughter, Miss Jill,' explained Mrs. Barrett. 'You know, the one that was so ill, and had to go and stay with her aunt in London . . . '

'Oh, yes, I know,' said Jill. 'What does she want to see me about?'

'I don't know — she won't say, miss,' said the housekeeper. 'But she won't go away . . . '

'All right, I'll come and see her . . . '

'Why not ask her to come in here?' suggested Gale.

'All right — bring her in here, then, Mrs. Barrett.'

'Yes, Miss Jill.'

She withdrew and when she returned in a moment or so she was accompanied by a plain-faced, rather nervous girl, who started fumbling with a handkerchief, and staring at the floor.

'Here's Agnes Potter, Miss Jill,' said Barrett.

'Well, Agnes,' said Jill. 'What do you want to see me about?'

'I 'ope you'll excuse the liberty me comin' 'ere like this, Miss 'Allam,' said

Agnes, unhappily. 'But mother said as it would be all right, an' that I ought to tell you . . . ' Her voice faded to incoherence and she cleared her throat.

'Tell me what, Agnes?' asked Jill.

Agnes looked as though she wished she hadn't come. With an effort she managed to find her voice again.

'I'd been to a dance over at Harchester, you see, miss, an' 'avin' to walk 'ome in the rain, I caught cold an' it turned to pneumonia.' She rushed into words, nervously. 'They thought I wasn't going to get better, an' when I did I was very weak-like, you see, an' mother said I ought to 'ave a change an' so I went to auntie's I didn't think anythin' of it until I came to see mother yesterday an' she told me about it might not have been Mrs. 'Allam after all, an' then I remembered what I'd seen . . . '

'What you'd *seen*?' said Jill, seizing on one sentence from this spate of words.

'On me way 'ome from the dance, yer see?' explained Agnes.

'Just a minute, Agnes,' said Gale. 'Don't go so fast. When did you go to this dance? Was it on the night that Mr. Hallam was killed?'

'Yes, sir — at least mother says it was. You see I was so ill I don't rightly know . . .'

'You walked back from this dance, and you saw something that you think we ought to know?' said Gale.

Agnes nodded.

'Yes, sir,' she said. 'That's why I come round 'ere . . .'

'What time was it when you came back from the dance?' asked Gale.

'Oh, it was very late, sir,' said Agnes. 'If I 'adn't been took ill like I was, there'd 'ave been a proper row with mother . . .'

'Yes, yes, I expect there would,' he said. 'But what time was it?'

'I 'eard the church clock strikin' two, sir, as I come past Easton Knoll . . .'

'And then you saw something — what did you see?'

Agnes licked her lips which seemed to have gone very dry.

'I saw someone leavin' the 'ouse, sir,' she answered. 'They was just comin' out o' the gates, sir, as I come along the lane . . . '

'Who was it, Agnes?' asked Jill. 'Could you see?'

'Yes, miss. Yer see it 'ad been dark up to then, but the moon come out just as I got in sight o' the drive. It was only fer a minute, an' then it clouded over again, but I see who it was all right . . . '

'Who was it, Agnes?' said Simon Gale.

'It was Mr. Upcott, sir,' she answered.

12

I

'That's the girl's story,' said Simon Gale to Inspector Frost half-an-hour later, 'and she's prepared to swear it was Robert Upcott.'

Frost took a bite from a wedge of cake and washed it down with a drink of tea. Gale had disturbed him in the middle of his meal.

'I'd be inclined to take 'er word for it, Mr. Gale,' he said. 'Agnes Potter wouldn't be likely to make a mistake. She's lived 'ere all 'er life, an' she's a steady, trustworthy sort o' girl. I wish we'd heard about this before, an' that's a fact . . . '

'You probably would have done if she hadn't caught pneumonia and been seriously ill at the time,' said Gale. 'She only came home today from her aunt's in London. When she heard her mother talking about what we were trying to do, she remembered . . . '

'It might 'ave made all the difference if we'd known earlier,' said Frost, frowning into the mug of tea, 'still it may be in time now. You know, ever since you first came an' told me you thought Mrs. 'Allam was innocent, I've had an idea in the back o' my mind that it might be Upcott . . . '

'Well, it certainly looks as though you were right, Inspector,' said Gale.

''E's a queer sort of feller, an' that's a fact — just the kind you'd expect to use poison if 'e wanted to get rid of someone . . . '

'No . . . not quite the kind *I* should expect,' said Gale, shaking his head, 'but it seems I'm wrong. Well, what are we going to do about this?'

'I think it ought to be followed up at once, sir,' said Frost.

'I agree,' said Gale, 'but who's going to do the following up? Look here, Inspector, I've an idea that I can get more out of Upcott than you. Don't misunderstand me — I don't doubt your ability — but you're rather restricted by red-tape, aren't you? You've got to be careful what you say to him, otherwise you may get hauled over the coals by your superiors . . . '

Frost considered this while he cut himself another wedge of cake.

'Well, there's somethin' in that, sir,' he said at last, 'an' that's a fact. These rules an' regulations don't make it too easy . . . '

'Exactly — but they don't apply to me,' said Simon, 'so suppose you let me tackle Upcott first? You can take over later.'

'It might be an idea, sir.'

'Right!' Gale got up and went over to the door. 'I'll go along and see him now . . . '

'Oh, Mr. Gale . . . ' Frost called to him as he was going out.

'Yes?'

'D'you think Rigg saw Upcott too, that night — an' that's what 'e was goin' to tell you?'

'Possibly — if it was, that would clinch things, wouldn't it?'

'Yes, sir,' said Frost.

II

Once more Gale stood outside the neat front door of Robert Upcott's house. Once more it was opened by Upcott himself who greeted him with his usual effusiveness.

'Come in — *do* come in,' he cried. 'I am so sorry to have kept you waiting, but I was in the kitchen preparing my evening meal . . . I adore cooking . . . '

'Sorry,' said Gale. 'if I'm disturbing you . . . '

'Don't apologize — *please* don't apologize.' Upcott led the way into the drawing-room. 'I'm always delighted to welcome a friend . . . '

'I don't want to spoil your dinner . . . '

'It can wait — I assure you it can wait. A *Chicken a la Casserole* — it will improve by keeping. Unless I can persuade you to join me? Can I — say I can . . . ?'

'No, no, thank you, Upcott,' said Gale. 'It's a little early for me . . . '

'Ah, yes, I understand,' said Upcott. 'Alas, I have to dine at this uncivilized hour. Otherwise I shouldn't sleep. I am a martyr to indigestion — a *martyr* . . . '

'I thought you took barbitone to make you sleep?' said Gale.

'I do — but I try not to make a *habit* of it,' replied Upcott. 'It's so degrading to have to depend on *drugs* in any form, I think. You agree — I'm sure you agree?'

'I want to have a little talk to you, Upcott,' said Gale, seriously.

Upcott clapped his plump hands in an ecstasy of pleasure.

'My dear sir, I'm always delighted to talk to someone of intelligence. The people round here' — he shrugged expressive shoulders — 'quite impossible, I assure you — quite impossible. It's such a *pleasure* to meet a broader mind, if you understand me . . . '

'I'm afraid this is rather — serious,' said Gale. 'Do you know Agnes Potter?'

'Agnes Potter?' Upcott made a grimace of distaste. 'Such a horrible name! Why *do* they have such *revolting* names? Really, I can't imagine . . . '

'You must know her . . . ?'

'Of *course* I know her,' declared

Upcott. 'In a village of this size, Mr. Gale, everybody knows everybody else. Agnes Potter is the daughter of a very worthy and respectable woman who takes in washing, but *what* has she to do with me?'

'She has a great deal to do with you. She says she saw you coming out of the gates of Easton Knoll on the night Hallam died . . . '

Robert Upcott's face went white, except for the rouge on the cheeks which stood out in grotesque patches so that he looked like a partly made-up clown.

'Really, how ridiculous,' he said. '*Surely* you don't believe such an outrageous statement? The girl must be *mad* . . . '

'I don't think she's mad at all,' said Gale.

'My dear sir,' protested Upcott, 'you cannot take this obviously absurd story seriously. I credit you with too much intelligence — far too much intelligence . . . '

'You deny that you were at Easton Knoll that night?'

'Absolutely!' declared Upcott. 'I was

nowhere near the place. What should I be doing there at two o'clock in the morning? It's fantastic — positively fantastic . . . '

'I didn't mention any *time*,' said Gale. 'What makes you think it was at two o'clock?'

Upcott was disconcerted. His eyes were restless with uneasiness and there was a faint tremor of his lower lip.

'I . . . I don't know . . . ' he said.

'I do,' said Gale, pressing home his advantage. 'It was because you heard the church clock strike two as you left Easton Knoll . . . '

'I wasn't at Easton Knoll that night,' asserted Upcott.

'It's no good lying,' said Gale. 'Agnes Potter is ready to swear — on oath, if necessary, that it *was* you . . . '

'She must have made a mistake . . . How could she be certain — in the dark? It's incredible . . . nobody would believe her . . . ' Upcott was slightly incoherent.

'*I* believe her,' said Gale. 'I think the police will, too.'

'It's not true,' said Upcott, desperately.

'You're trying to frighten me . . . you don't care who suffers as long as it isn't Margaret Hallam, and you're trying to fasten it on to me . . . '

'I'm not trying to fasten anything on to you,' retorted Gale. 'You were at Easton Knoll on the night that Hallam died, and I want to know why. It's no good trying to lie your way out of it — there's been too much lying by everybody — I want the truth and I mean to get it . . . '

'I've told you the truth . . . '

'What did Hallam know about you, Upcott?' demanded Gale.

'Nothing . . . nothing at all . . . '

'Oh, yes, he did. He knew something that you were so frightened he might divulge that you poisoned that whisky and milk. That's what you'd done when you crept away from Easton Knoll at two o'clock in the morning. John Hallam was *dead* then, wasn't he?'

'No . . . no, you're quite wrong, Gale . . . quite, quite wrong . . . '

'If he wasn't dead he was dying,' snapped Simon. 'Perhaps he wasn't dead

— barbitone takes quite a while to act . . . '

'I don't know anything about it . . . I had nothing to do with it . . . you've got to believe me . . . ' said Upcott entreatingly.

'It won't make much difference whether *I* believe you or not,' said Gale.

'What do you mean . . . ?'

'You surely don't imagine that this will rest with me?' said Gale. 'Of course it won't — it can't. This is fresh evidence that must be put before the police at once. They'll have to deal with it . . . '

'But it's all a mistake,' cried Upcott. 'Look here, Gale, it's all a mistake. I didn't kill Hallam — I swear to you I didn't . . . '

'You were there when he died, Upcott. Don't you see what that means? Nobody suspected that there was *anybody* at Easton Knoll that night, except Mrs. Hallam and the servants, until this girl, Agnes Potter came forward and said what she saw. It changes the whole circumstances. The police will have to take what action they think fit . . . '

'Listen . . . listen to me,' entreated Upcott. His face was a queer greenish colour and shining with sweat. 'I implore you not to bring the police into this . . . '

'You *were* at Easton Knoll that night?'

'Yes . . . yes, I was . . . but I can explain . . . I can explain everything. I didn't kill Hallam. He was already dead when I got there . . . '

'Do you seriously expect me to believe that?' said Gale.

'It's the truth . . . really it's the truth,' said Upcott. 'Hallam was dead in the chair. The empty glass was on the table by his side . . . '

'How do you know he was dead?' asked Gale.

'Because I — I touched him,' Upcott shuddered at the recollection. 'I thought at first he was asleep and — and I tried to wake him . . . '

'What time did you get there?'

'Half-past one,' Upcott was talking eagerly now, 'I went round to the French windows . . . He said he'd leave them unlatched . . . '

'Do you mean he was expecting you?'

'Yes, yes . . . I tried to see him during the day . . . '

'About the Doctor Wall teapot you were so anxious to possess?'

'No, no — that was just an excuse that I made to *you*. I wanted to see him about — something else. He wouldn't see me then . . . so I telephoned later. He — he told me if I liked to — to come about half-past one that night he'd leave the windows of the study unfastened . . . ' Upcott paused breathlessly.

'They were *fastened* when he was found in the morning,' said Gale.

'Yes, I know,' said Upcott. 'I fastened them — on the inside — before I left. I let myself out by the front door . . . It wasn't bolted . . . '

'Why did you go to the trouble. Why didn't you leave by the way you came?'

'I didn't want anyone to think that . . . anybody *might* have — have come that way. I was so confused and — and upset, I hardly knew what I was doing. It was dreadful — dreadful . . . finding him like that . . . '

'But you didn't say anything when Mrs.

Hallam was arrested, although, if you'd come forward, it might have made a difference?'

'I thought she'd killed him,' declared Upcott. 'Don't you see? You *must* see. I found him dead — with that empty glass on the table . . . I was *sure* she'd killed him. There was no point in my coming forward. You understand — I'm sure you understand?'

'I understand,' said Simon Gale, sternly, 'that you were willing to let a woman *hang* sooner than tell the truth . . . '

'But she's guilty — she *must* be guilty . . . '

'She's nothing of the kind . . . '

'But the glass was empty. Hallam had already drunk the poison. *She must* have been the one to give it him . . . '

'According to your story,' said Gale.

'It's the truth . . . I give you my word it's the truth . . . '

'What proof have you that it's the truth?'

'She gave him the whisky and milk just before midnight,' said Upcott eagerly.

'Would he have let it get cold . . . ?'

'There's only your word for the time you got to Easton Knoll,' Simon pointed out. 'Supposing it was earlier than you say — much earlier?'

'It wasn't . . . it was half-past one . . . '

'Well, supposing the poison *wasn't* administered in the whisky and milk after all?'

'But . . . '

'There was barbitone found in the dregs? Yes, I know. But *you* could have put that there, couldn't you? *After* you'd poisoned Hallam some other way — so that suspicion would fall on Mrs. Hallam . . . '

'You can't twist things like that . . . you can't,' cried Upcott. 'I've told you what happened — everything . . . '

'Not everything . . . Why were you so anxious to see Hallam?'

'I wanted to — to talk something over with him . . . '

'Hell's bells!' burst out Gale angrily. 'Stop trying to hide things, Upcott! It's too late for that. Hallam found out something about you, didn't he? The

247

same as he found out things about *other* people? Only in your case it was something *really* serious — something that frightened you into a panic. What did he know? What had you done?'

'It was nothing — nothing very important . . . '

'Nothing very important?' echoed Gale. 'Do you take me for a half-wit, Upcott? Nothing very important that made you try and see him during the day, and, when he wouldn't see you then, made you telephone and fix an appointment for *half-past one in the morning* . . . '

'I've told you all I'm going to,' said Upcott with a sudden burst of feeble temper. 'I won't say any more . . . you hear, I won't say any more . . . '

'If you don't say it now, you'll say it in a witness-box . . . '

'They can't do anything to me . . . I haven't done anything . . . '

'Can't they?' Gale laughed. 'You'll see what they can do. Are you going to tell me why you went to see Hallam that night?'

'Let me alone . . . ' cried Upcott almost in tears. 'Let me alone . . . I'm not feeling well . . . my nerves are all in rags . . . '

'Was it,' said Gale, trying a shot in the dark. 'Was it something that concerned — your wife?'

The shot went home. He could see that by the expression of Upcott's face, although he tried to hide it.

'No, no . . . it wasn't anything to do with her . . . How could it be?'

'Your wife ran away and left you, didn't she?' said Gale. 'She ran away with an unknown man, and you've never seen or heard from her since. That's right, isn't it?'

'Yes — yes, that's right . . . '

'Are you *sure*, Upcott?'

'What do you mean — what do you mean,' panted Upcott, and there was sheer panic in his eyes.

'Are you sure you never knew who the man was?'

To Gale's surprise the panic faded. Relief took its place.

'Yes . . . I never knew,' said Upcott. 'Please let me alone . . . I'm not in — in a fit state to answer any more questions . . . '

'Do you think Mrs. Hallam was in a fit state to answer all the questions *she* had to?' said Gale relentlessly. 'How do you think *she* felt, standing in the dock and listening to all the evidence piling up against her? How do you think she felt when she was found guilty and the Judge pronounced her death sentence . . . '

'I can't stand any more,' cried Upcott, hysterically. 'I tell you, I can't stand any more . . . '

'Then tell me the *whole* truth. *What was it Hallam knew?*'

'No, no, no!' Upcott began to sob wildly, uncontrollably. 'I can't tell you . . . '

'It was something to do with your wife, wasn't it? She left you and you've never seen her since — nobody's seen or heard of her . . . '

A sudden thought struck him like the sudden flashing on of a light in a dark room.

'Upcott — *did* she ever run away? Was

there *any* man — known or unknown . . . ?'

'Yes, yes — of course there was . . . I don't know what you mean . . . '

'I mean,' said Simon Gale, '*did your wife ever leave this house?*'

13

I

'Is that it, Upcott?' said Simon Gale. 'Was the story you told to account for the disappearance of your wife a lie?'

'No . . . no . . . ' moaned Upcott. 'No . . . '

'What happened to your wife, Upcott?' persisted Gale.

'Nothing, I tell you . . . nothing . . . I don't know what you mean . . . '

'Did you poison *her* too?'

'No . . . ' Upcott put his hands up to his head. 'Oh, stop it . . . stop it, do you hear . . . ?'

'Tell me the truth, Upcott . . . '

'I didn't . . . poison anybody . . . '

Upcott was almost at breaking point. Gale felt reluctant to press him further but he forced himself to continue his verbal third degree. After all, Margaret's life was at stake.

'What *did* you do?'

'Leave me alone . . . leave me alone . . . ' whispered Upcott. 'I . . . I haven't done anything . . . '

'All right,' snapped Gale. 'If you'd prefer that the police . . . '

He went over to the telephone.

'No . . . ' Upcott gripped his arm with trembling fingers. 'Stop . . . leave that telephone alone . . . I'll . . . I'll tell you . . . It was an accident . . . We — we quarrelled . . . I pushed her and . . . she fell . . . She struck her head . . . on the corner of the table . . . ' He shuddered.

'It killed her?' asked Gale.

'Yes . . . yes, she was dead . . . ' Upcott swallowed with difficulty. 'I thought — I thought people would . . . say I'd done it . . . '

'So you hid the body and told everyone she'd run away?' said Gale.

'I was mad . . . I didn't realize what I was doing . . . '

Gale eyed him keenly.

'You're quite sure you didn't kill her?' he said.

'Yes . . . It was an accident . . . I swear

it was an accident . . . '

'Hallam found out?'

'He suspected . . . he didn't *know* . . . he threatened to have inquiries made . . . '

'And so,' said Simon Gale, 'you poisoned him to keep him quiet . . . ?'

'No, no, no!' screamed Upcott, a fleck of foam appearing on his lips. 'You're wrong — wrong — I . . . I . . . I . . . '

He choked, uttered a little groaning cry, and collapsed on the floor at Gale's feet.

'Hell's bells,' muttered Gale. He bent down, but Upcott was quite unconscious and breathing heavily. He looked very bad and Gale went quickly to the telephone.

'Hello . . . ' he called and when the operator answered: 'Get me Doctor Evershed . . . No, I don't know the number, but it's very urgent . . . yes, be quick please . . . '

'This is an eye-opener, an' that's a fact,' declared Inspector Frost. It was half-an-hour later and he and Gale were sitting in Robert Upcott's ornate drawing-room.

'It is rather,' said Simon. 'When he collapsed in the fit, or whatever it was, I telephoned Evershed and then you. Evershed's upstairs with him now.'

Frost shook his head.

'We never suspected anythin' of the sort,' he said. 'But I don't 'ave to tell you that. Mind you, I always thought that Upcott knew more about 'is wife's runnin' away than 'e let on, but I thought it was just the name o' the man 'e was concealin' — I never dreamed there was anythin' like this . . .'

'Apparently Hallam was wiser,' said Gale.

'Yes, sir, you're right,' agreed Frost. 'Of course, Mr. and Mrs. Upcott never 'it it off — everybody knew *that* — but, well, you'd never think he was the kind of chap to do a thing like that . . .'

'I don't agree with you there,' said

Gale. 'I think he's just the sort of chap to act exactly as he did. He's neurotic, excitable, very liable to panic . . . oh, yes, I think he'd behave *just* like that . . . '

'Do you believe 'is story, then? That 'is wife's death was an accident?' asked Frost.

'Yes, I think it's quite plausible,' answered Simon. 'Faced with that situation he'd do just what he says he did. He was scared. He thought he'd be accused of killing her. He had no proof to show it was an accident. Supposing he'd come to you — would you have believed him?'

The Inspector considered for a moment.

'Well, no,' he answered, at length, 'it would have taken a bit of swallowin', sir.'

'There you are, you see?' said Gale. 'Nor would anybody else. He was right there. Even if he hadn't been found guilty of murder, the suspicion would always have stuck. From his point of view he did the only thing possible . . . '

'Well, we shall have to find the body before we can take any action,' said Frost.

'He didn't say what 'e'd done with . . . ?'

'No, I've no more idea than you. That'll have to wait until he recovers.'

'It gives him a pretty strong motive for gettin' 'Allam out of the way, sir,' said Frost, after a pause.

'Yes — I suppose it does,' said Gale.

'There's not much doubt in my opinion, sir,' went on the Inspector, ''E was there that night, we've got a witness for that, an' if 'Allam suspected the truth about Mrs. Upcott — well, naturally Upcott 'ud want to stop 'im talkin' . . . '

'And Rigg too,' put in Gale, 'don't forget that, Inspector. The person who killed Hallam, killed Rigg . . . '

'Yes, of course, sir,' said Frost. 'Rigg saw Upcott leavin' Easton Knoll — the same as Agnes Potter did. That's clear enough . . . '

'Is it clear enough to stop Mrs. Hallam being hanged on Friday morning?' said Gale.

'It ought to be,' said Frost. 'I shall get on to the Chief Constable first thing in the morning — I've got to report this other business anyway . . . '

'I don't think you'll find it's so easy to get them to do anything about Mrs. Hallam, Frost,' Gale shook his head. 'There's still no real evidence, you know . . . '

'Unless we can get a confession out of Upcott . . . ' He stopped and looked round as Doctor Evershed came in. 'Hello, doctor — 'ow is he?'

'He's still unconscious.'

'What is it?'

'A stroke,' said Evershed. He took out his case and lit a cigarette.

'Will 'e recover?' asked Frost.

'He may,' Evershed blew out a cloud of smoke. 'He'll need care. I shall have to arrange for a nurse, or get him to a hospital . . . '

'How long is it likely to be before he's able to talk?' said Frost.

'I can't tell. There's a cerebral haemorrhage. Even if he recovers consciousness, he'll have to be kept very quiet. Any kind of excitement might be fatal. What brought on the seizure?'

'I was asking him some rather awkward questions,' said Gale, 'he got very worked

258

up, and suddenly collapsed. I didn't like the look of him, so I phoned for you . . . '

'I thought he'd had some kind of shock,' Evershed nodded. 'What was it — the Hallam business?'

'Yes.'

'Is he seriously involved?'

'Yes, I think he is . . . '

'It's important that we should be able to take a statement from 'im as soon as possible, doctor,' said Frost. 'Mrs. 'Allam's life may depend on what 'e can tell us.'

'Like that is it?' Evershed inhaled deeply. 'Well, I'll do my best for you, but I can't promise anything. At present it's touch and go . . . '

There was a knock on the front door.

'Who's that?' grunted Gale.

'I don't know. Some friend of Upcott's, I suppose . . . ' said Evershed.

'I'll go,' said Frost.

He hurried into the hall and opened the front door. Miss Ginch stood on the doorstep.

'I was passing and I saw the light, so I thought . . . Oh . . . Inspector Frost . . . '

'Come in, Miss Ginch,' said the Inspector.

'But I don't understand,' said Miss Ginch, peering inquisitively about her. 'I called to see Mr. Upcott. What are *you* doing here, Inspector? Oh, dear me, *and* Doctor Evershed and Mr. Gale — really, I don't understand at *all*. Where is Mr. Upcott?'

'I'm afraid you won't be able to see Mr. Upcott, Miss Ginch,' said Gale.

'Why not,' said Miss Ginch. 'Oh, *do* tell me what has happened? Surely he hasn't been *arrested* . . . '

'Why should you think that, miss?' said Frost.

'Well, *you're* here, Inspector, and I was talking to Mrs. Potter a little while ago, and *she* said that her daughter, Agnes . . . '

'And you thought you'd come and see if there was any truth in what she said, is that it, Miss Ginch?' said Gale.

'Well, of course, one naturally takes an *interest*,' said Miss Ginch. 'I'm sure the whole *village* is only too *eager* to know what is going to happen to poor Margaret

Hallam. So terrible for her, poor thing, and the time going by so *quickly*. Yes, indeed. There's only tomorrow, isn't there, and nothing really *definite* . . . '

'You can supply the whole village with a *really* definite piece of news, Miss Ginch,' broke in Evershed sarcastically. 'Upcott has had a stroke and is very seriously ill . . . '

'Oh, Doctor Evershed, how very, very shocking . . . ' Miss Ginch's eyes glistened with interest.

'I'm quite sure any shock you may feel will be amply compensated by the supreme pleasure it will afford you to retail such a choice tit-bit, Miss Ginch,' said Evershed.

'Really — *really*, Doctor Evershed,' said Miss Ginch. 'That is a most unkind and *unchristian* thing to say. Anyone would *imagine* that I enjoyed such things . . . '

'It wouldn't necessitate a *very* great effort of imagination,' snapped Evershed.

'Doctor Evershed,' said Miss Ginch, her cheeks burning, 'you've no right to speak to me like that . . . '

'Possibly I haven't,' he retorted, 'but I detest cant and humbug . . . '

'Oh . . . '

'Before I came here, Miss Ginch,' he went on, 'I had a practice in Wimbourne. Perhaps that conveys something to you — it should do . . . '

Miss Ginch stared at him, her lips parted and her face blanched.

'Wimbourne,' she whispered in a voice that was slightly cracked.

'Perhaps you didn't know that?' he went on 'I think you *did*. I think that's why you have always disliked me so much. I have a more tangible reason for disliking you . . . I'm going upstairs to look at my patient . . . '

He walked quickly and angrily to the door and went out.

'Oh,' said Miss Ginch, in a sudden flutter, 'Oh, really, I can't think *what* he can mean . . . oh, dear, I — I feel quite overcome . . . '

'Sit down here, Miss Ginch,' said Gale.

'Oh, thank you . . . Doctor Evershed is so brusque and *ill-mannered* . . . '

'*Have* you ever been to Wimbourne,

Miss Ginch?' asked Gale.

'No — no indeed . . . never . . . '

'The mention of it conveys nothing to you, then?'

'Nothing at all,' declared Miss Ginch.

'Are you quite sure of that, Miss Ginch?' said Gale.

She looked at him with tight lips.

'I am *not* in the habit of lying, Mr. Gale . . . '

'Perhaps not as a *habit*,' he said. 'Would it be wrong to suggest that this is the exception . . . ?'

'Really — I don't know in the least what you are talking about . . . oh, dear,' said Miss Ginch, plaintively, 'I feel a little faint . . . '

'I'll get you a glass of water, miss,' said Frost.

'It's very kind of you, but I think, perhaps, fresh air would be more beneficial,' said Miss Ginch. 'It really is very hot in here . . . ' She got up and went over to the door. 'I'm afraid you'll have to excuse me. Please don't trouble . . . I can let myself out . . . '

They heard the front door open and

shut, and looked at each other.

'Well, sir, what do you think o' that?' said Frost. 'Somethin' shook 'er up, an' that's a fact . . . '

'There's no mystery about it,' said Gale. 'She knew what Doctor Evershed was alluding to when he mentioned Wimbourne, but I don't think she was aware *he* knew until tonight. That's what shook her . . . '

'She's always 'ad it in for the doctor — ever since 'e came here,' said Frost, 'I told you that, sir. Very spiteful about 'im . . . '

'Murder's a queer thing, Frost,' said Simon Gale. 'It's like suddenly turning on a bright light in an old, damp cellar. All kinds of nasty, crawling things go scuttling away to their holes to get out of the glare . . . '

'You're right, sir. This place seems to 'ave more than a fair share . . . '

'Oh, I wouldn't say that,' said Gale. 'I think you'd find the same thing anywhere. Everybody's got something to hide, but normally it *remains* hidden. It's only when something like murder happens, and blows all the secret places wide open, that the skeletons come to life . . . '

Evershed came in.

'There's no change,' he said. 'Upcott's still unconscious.' He looked round. 'Has that Ginch woman gone?'

'Yes,' said Gale. 'What do you know about her, Evershed?'

'I don't know that I ought to tell you,' said Evershed. 'Normally I *wouldn't* tell you. Malicious gossip's not in my line . . . '

'It's your duty to tell us anything you know, doctor,' said Frost.

'All right — but there's no need to let it go any further,' said Evershed. 'Unless, of course, it's absolutely necessary . . . '

'I can promise you that, sir.'

'Well, then, this is it. I was called out one night at Wimbourne — urgent call. A woman had tried to gas herself. She lived in one room in a slum — a filthy place with scarcely any furniture — and she owed a month's rent. The landlady was turning her out. I was able to bring her round, though I think it would have been kinder to have let her die. She was half-starved and both lungs were badly tubercular — she couldn't have lived long in any case. I got her into hospital, but she died three days later. Her name was — Ginch . . . '

'What — relation?' asked Gale.

'Younger sister,' Evershed thrust his hands into his pockets and sat down on the arm of an easy chair. 'She told me all about herself before she died. Nothing new — old as the hills. Too strict upbringing with the result that she kicked over the traces . . . There was a child which died at birth . . . Her parents and the sister threw her out . . . She went on the streets and eventually reached the condition in which I first found her. Sordid story — like a good many others. Here's the point. She wanted to see her sister before she died. She wrote to her. I posted the letter and registered it to make sure. Miss Ginch didn't even bother to reply. That's all.'

'I never knew she 'ad a sister,' said Frost.

'She didn't come to live here until after her parents were dead, did she?' said Evershed. 'She wouldn't mention her sister *then*. It would never do for it to become known that she was related to a woman who 'was no better than she should be'. What would the 'Christian Mothers' Guild' say to that?' He shrugged his shoulders. 'Can you wonder that the sight of her, with all her sanctimonious hypocrisy, makes me want to vomit?'

'I wonder,' remarked Simon Gale, after a pause, 'if Hallam knew?'

'I hope so,' said Evershed viciously. 'I hope he made her squirm with fear that he might give her away. She's a poisonous female . . .'

'That might be a better description than you imagine, Evershed,' said Gale.

III

The telephone bell rang loudly and shrilly at Easton Knoll, and Jill picked up the receiver.

'Easton Knoll,' she said. 'Oh, good

267

morning, Inspector Frost . . . Yes, he's here. Hold on, will you? Inspector Frost wants to speak to you, Simon . . . '

He came over and took the telephone receiver from her.

'Hello, Frost,' he said. 'Oh, is he . . . well, I hope he's successful . . . you'll let me know at once, won't you? . . . Yes . . . How's Upcott? . . . I see . . . Yes, I wonder if you could let me know? I should like to be there, if possible . . . yes, do . . . all right . . . goodbye . . . '

He dropped the receiver back on the rack.

'The Chief Constable is ringing up the Home Office to see if they will grant a stay of execution, pending further inquiries,' he said.

'Do you think they will?' asked Jill anxiously.

He shrugged his shoulders.

'They ought to,' he answered. 'We've definite proof that Upcott came here that night. Whether that's sufficient for them to act on, I don't know . . . '

'Surely it will be, Simon,' she said. 'It must be . . . '

'There's no surely about it,' he answered. 'Frost sounded rather dubious. If we could get a statement out of Upcott it might help, although he swears that Hallam was either dead, or dying, when he got here . . . '

'Is it likely he'd say anything else?' she demanded.

'No, but the evidence of the whisky and milk is in his favour. Maggie took Hallam that drink before midnight. Agnes Potter saw Upcott at two o'clock, just leaving. If he got there in time to put the poison in the whisky and milk before Hallam drank it, it must have been round about twelve o'clock — the drink was hot, remember. Hallam wouldn't have waited for it to get cold. Why the deuce should Upcott have hung about for nearly two hours after he'd administered the poison? It doesn't make sense — the risk of someone finding him was pretty great . . . '

'Unless he wanted to make sure the poison had taken effect,' said Jill.

'He wouldn't have had to wait all that time,' said Gale. 'Hallam would have been in a coma in a very short time after

swallowing that amount of barbitone.
. . .'

'There must have been *some* reason, Simon. I'm sure it was Upcott — it must have been. Look at the motive he had . . . '

'I'll admit *that's* strong enough,' he agreed. 'Perhaps we shall know more about it when he recovers consciousness . . . '

'When is that likely?'

'Evershed told Frost it might be any moment. They've got a nurse with him, and Frost has put a man with instructions to telephone immediately there's any sign of his coming round . . . '

Mrs. Barrett came in.

'Will you see Miss Lane and Mrs. Langdon-Humphreys?' she asked.

Jill looked surprised.

'Oh, yes,' she answered. 'Ask them to come in . . . Now what do *they* want so early in the morning,' she said when the housekeeper had gone.

'I should say that they'd heard about Upcott,' remarked Gale, 'and want to know more — and it's *not* so early, Jill.

270

It's half-past nine . . . '

'It's early for those two,' said Jill.

They came in quickly, scarcely pausing for the usual greetings before they came to the object of their visit.

'We've just heard about Mr. Upcott,' said Vanessa.

'Is it true?' demanded Mrs. Langdon-Humphreys.

'Yes, he had a seizure last night,' said Gale.

'I don't mean *that*,' said Mrs. Langdon-Humphreys. 'Is it true that he murdered his wife?'

'And poisoned Mr. Hallam?' added Vanessa.

'Where did you hear that?' asked Gale.

'It's all round the village . . . ' began Vanessa.

'Never mind that,' interrupted Mrs. Langdon-Humphreys impatiently. 'The question is, is it true?'

'I'm afraid I can't tell you,' said Gale.

'Why not?' she demanded.

'Because I don't know,' he answered. 'According to Upcott the death of his wife was an accident . . . '

271

'Then she *did* die?' said Vanessa. 'She didn't run away as everyone thought . . . ?'

'No, she died,' replied Gale.

'Robert Upcott was seen leaving here on the night Mr. Hallam died,' said Mrs. Langdon-Humphreys. 'That girl Potter saw him . . . '

'That is also true,' said Gale. 'And that is all we actually *know* . . . '

'Well, it seems to me very obvious that he must be the person who poisoned John Hallam,' declared Mrs. Langdon-Humhpreys. 'If he had found out that Upcott's wife never ran away . . . '

'Upcott would have had a strong motive?' finished Gale. 'Yes, I agree with you . . . '

'This will make a difference to Margaret, won't it?' said Vanessa. 'I mean they won't go through with — with it now?'

'The Chief Constable is trying to get a stay of execution,' said Jill.

'They *must* do that, *mustn't* they?' asked Vanessa. 'Surely they can't . . . '

'If a stay of execution is granted it

would be tantamount to a reprieve,' said Simon Gale. 'Once a stay of execution is granted the execution is never carried out afterwards . . . '

'But that would be wonderful,' exclaimed Vanessa.

'I doubt if the Home Secretary will consider the evidence we can offer sufficient for that,' he said.

'If he doesn't, Simon,' said Jill. 'What are we going to do? It's tomorrow — tomorrow morning . . . '

'We can offer him evidence that he *will* consider sufficient,' said Gale.

'Have you such evidence, Mr. Gale?' asked Mrs. Langdon-Humphreys.

'Not at present,' he answered.

'Then how are you going to get it, Simon?' demanded Jill. 'There isn't any *time* . . . '

'I shall have it this afternoon,' he said, quietly.

They stared at him. His reply had been so unexpected that for a moment they were too astonished to speak.

'What's going to happen this afternoon?' said Vanessa, sharply.

'I hope you'll come and see?' he said. 'Could you both come to tea — say at four o' clock?'

'I've no doubt we could,' said Mrs. Langdon-Humphreys. 'If you could be a little more explicit as to why it should be necessary, my recollection of the *last* time we were invited here is not altogether a pleasant one . . . '

'I should like you to come,' said Gale, 'because I'm going to tell you who murdered John Hallam . . . '

'Simon!' exclaimed Jill.

'You — you know?' It was almost a whisper from Vanessa.

'Yes, I know,' said Gale.

'Are you quite sure, Mr. Gale?' asked Mrs. Langdon-Humphreys.

'Quite sure,' he answered.

'Who is it,' said Jill. 'Who is it, Simon . . . ?'

Before he could reply the telephone bell rang. With a word of excuse he went over to the instrument and lifted the receiver.

'Hello . . . speaking . . . oh, yes, yes . . . I'll come at once . . . ' He looked round.

'I'm afraid I must go,' he said. 'Upcott has just recovered consciousness . . . '

IV

'Come in, Gale,' said Doctor Evershed in a low voice, and ushered him into the darkened bedroom. 'Frost's here . . . '

Gale could dimly make out the figures of the Inspector and a nurse standing near the bed.

'What has Upcott said?' he asked.

'Nothing yet,' answered Evershed. 'He can't speak very easily. I've given him a slight stimulant . . . '

'He looks pretty bad, sir,' muttered Frost.

'He is,' said Evershed. 'If the circumstances were not as urgent, I wouldn't allow him to be disturbed. As it is you'll have to be very careful not to excite him . . . '

'Can I go over and speak to him?' asked Simon.

'Yes, but don't forget what I said . . . '

Gale went over to the bed. Upcott lay

275

back on his pillows. His face was deathly pale, and his eyes were only visible through half closed lids.

'Hello, Upcott,' said Gale, gently. 'How are you feeling?'

The dry-looking lips moved and a slight spasm contorted the mouth. Very faintly sounds, slurred and almost inaudible, shaped themselves into words:

'I . . . I . . . thirsty . . . '

'Drink a little of this?' Evershed held a glass to the sick man's lips. With great difficulty, Upcott swallowed a few drops. After a pause he spoke again. It was still an effort but his voice was a trifle stronger.

'What . . . what am . . . I . . . am I doing . . . here?'

'You were taken ill,' said Evershed, 'don't you remember?'

'Ill? . . . I . . . I've been . . . ill . . . ?'

'Yes.'

The fingers on the coverlet plucked at it. The head moved very slightly. The half-open eyes rested on Gale.

'Are . . . are . . . ' the slurred voice

failed and then went on: 'Are . . . you doctor . . . ?'

'No,' said Gale, 'Evershed's the doctor . . . you know Evershed . . . ?'

'Evershed . . . ?' repeated Upcott, but there was no recognition in his voice.

'That's right, Upcott,' said Evershed. 'Drink a little more of this . . . '

Upcott sipped a few drops.

'How . . . how long have . . . I been . . . been here?' he asked.

'Since yesterday evening,' said Gale.

'Yesterday . . . evening . . . ?'

'We were talking when you were taken ill . . . I'm Simon Gale . . . '

'Simon . . . Gale? . . . I . . . don't know . . . '

'You remember me, don't you? I was talking to you about Hallam . . . '

'Hallam . . . ? No . . . I don't . . . know . . . '

Evershed took Gale by the arm and led him away.

'It's no good, Gale,' he said, shaking his head. 'His memory's gone. He doesn't remember anything . . . '

14

I

'Do you mean, Simon, that his mind's a complete blank?' asked Jill.

'I'm afraid so,' said Gale, 'for the present at any rate Evershed says that he may recover his memory later . . . '

'What happens in the meanwhile?' asked Martin.

'Nothing so far as Upcott is concerned,' said Gale. 'It's useless questioning a man who can't remember . . . '

'Do you think it's genuine . . . ?' said Martin.

'Oh, yes, there's no doubt about that. He's being kept under observation — in case there should be any change.'

'Has there been any message from the Chief Constable?' said Jill.

'Not yet,' answered Gale. 'There's hardly been time. I'm not putting any hope in a stay of execution — particularly now there's no chance of getting a statement out of Upcott . . . '

'If you meant what you said this morning, it won't matter, will it?' said Jill. '*Did* you mean it, Simon?'

'I meant it, Jill,' said Gale.

'Meant what?' asked Martin.

'Simon says he knows who killed my father . . . '

'Is that true, Simon?' said Martin.

'Quite true . . . '

'Well, then, tell us — who was it?'

'I'll tell you this afternoon,' said Gale.

'Why can't you tell us now?' asked Jill.

'Because I can't, Jill,' he answered. 'There are very good reasons why I must wait until this afternoon . . . '

'I believe you're only saying that . . . '

'For dramatic effect?' he said, with a smile. 'No, I'm not, I assure you. Do you think I'd bother about that in the circumstances — with Maggie's life at stake? I've *got* to wait . . . '

'To make sure,' asked Martin.

'Yes — but not in the way you mean,' he answered.

'Surely you can give us some *hint*,

Simon,' persisted Jill.

'No, you'll have to be patient,' said Gale.

'Oh, you're maddening, Simon,' exclaimed Jill with sudden irritability. 'Don't you realize how much this means to — to all of us? Why must you behave like — like a detective in a book — keeping everything to yourself until the last chapter . . . '

'Steady, Jill,' said Gale, but she went on without heeding:

'That's all very well in a story, but *you're* dealing with real people — people with feelings and — and nerves . . . ' Her voice broke suddenly. 'Oh, can't you understand?'

She walked quickly to the door, opened it, and went out.

Martin looked at Simon and shrugged his shoulders.

'She's feeling the strain,' he said.

'She's been feeling the strain for a long time,' said his brother, going over and closing the door. 'You're partly to blame, Martin . . . '

'Me?' exclaimed Martin.

'You must be blind if you haven't seen it,' said Simon. 'Jill's in love with you . . . '

'Oh, heck!' said Martin in dismay.

'She as good as admitted it yesterday — not that it was necessary. You've only to watch her face when you and Vanessa are together . . . '

'Oh, Lord, Simon, this complicates things . . . '

'Not necessarily,' said Simon, quickly. 'You know what you've got to do?'

'It's all very well for you . . . '

'Hell's bells,' cried Simon irritably, 'don't be a fool! *I* know how you feel about Vanessa, but you've got to pull yourself together. It's useless . . . '

'Inspector Frost is here, sir,' said Mrs. Barrett from the doorway.

'Oh, ask him in,' said Gale.

The housekeeper withdrew and Simon turned to Martin.

'Now look,' he said, 'go and find Jill. Take her for a walk, talk to her . . . there's no need to upset yourself, everything will be all right . . . '

'I hope so,' grunted Martin. He nodded

to Frost as the latter was shown in. 'Where's Miss Jill, Mrs. Barrett?'

'I think she went upstairs, sir,' said the housekeeper.

'See you later, Simon,' said Martin and shut the door behind him.

'Well, Mr. Gale, I've just heard from the Chief Constable,' said Frost, when they were alone.

'Nothing doing, eh?' said Gale.

'If you cut out all the trimmin's, that's what it amounts to, sir . . . '

'I never expected anything else,' said Gale.

'If we could have got a statement out of Upcott . . . ' began Frost.

'Only a signed confession would have done any good, Inspector,' said Gale, 'and I don't think you'd have got that . . . '

'No, I don't s'pose 'e'd have been fool enough for that, sir, an' that's a fact. What are we goin' to do now — about Mrs. 'Allam . . . '

'Come round to tea this afternoon,' said Gale, 'and you'll see . . . '

Inspector Frost raised his eyebrows.

'If you've anything in mind, sir,' he

said, 'that'll be leavin' it a bit late, won't it?'

'Yes, but I can't help it, Frost,' said Gale. 'I can't do anything before.'

'What are you going to do then, sir?'

'I'm going to . . . ' Gale broke off as Jill came in quickly. She looked radiant.

'Martin's asked me to go for a walk, Simon,' she said, and then seeing Frost: 'Oh, good morning, Inspector . . . '

'Good morning, miss . . . '

'A walk's a very good idea, Jill,' said Gale. 'It'll cheer you up . . . '

'Is there any news?' she asked.

'The Home Secretary won't do anything . . . '

'Oh . . . ' The happiness faded from her face.

'Never mind,' said Gale, 'you go along for your walk . . . and Jill — keep Martin away as long as possible . . . '

'Why?' she asked.

'You'll know why this afternoon,' he said.

She looked at him searchingly.

'Simon . . . ' she began.

'Are you ready, Jill?' called Martin from the hall.

'Yes, coming now, Martin,' she called back and then lowering her voice: 'All right, Simon, I think I understand . . .'

She hurried away.

Simon Gale went over and carefully shut the door. Coming back, he sat down and took out his pipe.

'Now, Frost,' he said, 'listen to me — and don't interrupt until I've finished . . .'

II

'Here's your dinner, Hallam,'

The wardress set down the tray in front of Margaret.

'Thank you,' she said, listlessly.

'The chaplain's coming down to see you,' said the woman.

'Oh, has there been a message?' asked Margaret eagerly.

The wardress shook her head.

'I don't know,' she answered.

'I expect that's what it is,' said

Margaret. 'It's not his usual time, is it?'

'No, but he hasn't been to see you before, today. If it was anything special, the Governor would have come . . . '

The light died out of Margaret's eyes.

'Yes . . . I suppose so . . . '

There was a tap on the cell door, and the other wardress turned the key and opened it. The Chaplain came in quickly.

'Good morning, Mrs. Hallam,' he said. 'I'm afraid I've chosen a bad moment. You're just going to have your luncheon . . . I'll come back later . . . '

'No, please stay,' she said, quickly. 'I'm not — very hungry . . . '

'You didn't eat your breakfast,' said the wardress.

'Come now, Mrs. Hallam,' said the Chaplain, 'you must try and eat, you know . . . '

'Have you — have you anything to tell me?' asked Margaret.

'You've heard nothing from your friends?' inquired the Chaplain.

She shook her head.

'No, nothing . . . '

He looked grave.

'It was a very difficult task,' he said.

'Yes . . . the miracle isn't going to happen this time,' she said.

'You mustn't give up hope, Mrs. Hallam,' he said.

'I'm trying not to,' her voice was not quite steady, 'but — the time's getting very short now, isn't it? This — this is — the last day . . . '

He saw that she was on the verge of a breakdown, and laid his hand gently on her arm.

'You've been very brave . . . you mustn't give way now . . . '

'Simon was . . . so sure,' she said, 'so *confident* . . . that it would be all right . . . He couldn't just have been *saying* that . . . '

'Nobody would be so cruel as that,' said the Chaplain soothingly. 'There's nothing worse than raising — false hopes. I tried to warn you to be prepared . . . '

'I know . . . I know,' she whispered, the tears gathering in her eyes, 'but I did think . . . I was so *sure* . . . '

'There's still time, you know,' he said. 'I don't think I'm guilty of raising false hopes by saying that . . . '

'I haven't . . . any hope . . . now . . . '
She suddenly burst into an uncontrollable
fit of sobbing . . .

'Mrs. Hallam . . . ' he began in
concern.

'I don't want to die,' she cried brokenly.
'I don't . . . want to die . . . '

III

'There you are, Frost,' said Simon Gale,
tapping out the ashes from his pipe. 'Now
you know all about it.'

The Inspector's face was a study in
astonishment.

'Well, sir,' he declared drawing a long
breath, 'you've properly surprised *me*, an'
that's a fact . . . '

'You see, now, why I can't do anything
until this afternoon?' said Gale.

Frost nodded slowly.

'Yes, I see that, sir,' he said. 'Even then
it's a bit of a gamble, isn't it?'

'Of course it is, but what else can I do?
Although I *know* that what I have told

you it's the *truth*, I've no proof . . . '

'That letter that was s'posed to 'ave come from Rigg . . . ?' suggested Frost.

Gale shrugged his shoulders.

'I don't think that would be sufficient,' he said. 'There's only one way of getting proof — absolute and convincing proof — and that's the way I've outlined . . . '

'I agree with you, sir — if it works,' said the Inspector, doubtfully.

'I think it will,' said Gale. 'It's a question of psychology . . . It would be in character, you know.'

'Well, sir, that'd be something you know more about than me, an' that's a fact. I only 'ope you're right . . . '

'It depends on a very slender thread,' Gale picked up a piece of string that was lying on a table near him, 'much less strong than this. But I think we shall pull it off. I believe the opportunity will be too great for the murderer to resist . . . '

'It's going to be pretty dangerous, sir, if anything goes wrong,' said Frost.

'But *I'm* the one who takes the risk,' said Gale.

'Yes, I s'pose that's true . . . ' Frost got

up. 'I must be gettin' along,' he said. 'We've got to try an' find what Upcott did with the body of 'is wife . . . '

'Is Upcott still at the house?'

'No, they've taken him to the cottage hospital. Couldn't, very well 'ave 'im there while we was conductin' the search . . . '

'It seems rather lucky for him that he had that stroke,' said Gale. 'He won't know anything about it . . . '

'That's a fact, sir, but it's goin' to give us a lot of extra trouble . . . '

'Man was born to trouble,' said Gale. 'I've realized the truth of that in the last few days. You won't be late this afternoon?'

'No, sir — 'alf-past four . . . '

'Make it a little earlier, if you can manage it . . . '

'All right, sir . . . '

Frost had his hand on the door handle, when it was opened by Mrs. Barrett.

'Excuse me, sir. Major Fergusson wants to see you . . . '

'Fergusson?' said Gale.

'I've put him in the study, sir . . . '

'Ask him to come in here, Mrs. Barrett . . . '

'Yes, sir,' she nodded and went away.

'I wonder what Fergusson wants, sir?' said Frost.

Simon Gale fiddled with the piece of string, twisting and turning it about in his sensitive fingers.

'I'm rather wondering that, Inspector . . . '

'Well, I'll 'ave to go, Mr. Gale,' said Frost. He opened the door. 'Goodbye — I'll see you this afternoon, sir . . . '

'Major Fergusson, sir,' announced Mrs. Barrett.

Fergusson came in. He looked white and strained and ill. Gale thought he probably hadn't slept very much recently.

'Good morning, Mr. Gale,' he spoke jerkily and the muscles about his mouth were twitching. 'I . . . hope I'm not disturbing you, but there was something I wanted to see you about . . . ' His eyes, moving restlessly, fastened on the string that Simon was playing with. 'What are you doing?' he said. 'What are you doing with that string . . . ?'

Gale looked down at his hands. He hadn't realized what he was doing and when he saw he started.

'Quite unconsciously I seem to have been fashioning — a noose . . . ' he said.

15

I

Mrs. Barrett uttered a little gasp. Her eyes were staring in horror. She said in a strangled voice:

'A noose . . . '

'Not a very pleasant thing to fashion, Mr. Gale,' said Fergusson.

'No . . . the subconscious mind plays strange tricks, doesn't it?' said Gale. 'I'd no idea I'd made a noose. I was just fiddling about with this string while I was talking to Inspector Frost . . . '

'It's . . . it's horrible . . . ' gulped Mrs. Barrett, 'horrible . . . ' She went out quickly, shutting the door with a little thud.

'She seems to be quite upset?' muttered Fergusson.

'Yes — an association of ideas, perhaps,' Gale threw the string into the fire. 'Sit down, Fergusson . . . '

'Thank you. I — I came to ask if there was anything definite yet?'

'About Hallam's murder?'

'Yes — you see it's worrying me,' Fergusson moistened his lips with the tip of his tongue. 'I can't get the thought of that poor woman — just waiting and waiting — out of my mind. The time's getting very close, now . . .'

'Very close,' agreed Gale.

'Can you not do anything? I've heard about Upcott, and I wondered . . .'

'If he killed Hallam?'

'Yes.'

'Are you interested to know who killed Hallam, Fergusson?' asked Gale.

'Do you know?' said Fergusson sharply.

'Yes,' said Gale.

'Who?'

'If you care to come here this afternoon, I'll tell you . . .'

'But, man, if you know, why wait?' demanded Fergusson. 'The execution's fixed for the morning — why don't you have the murderer arrested, and get Mrs. Hallam released at once . . . ?'

'There are reasons — very good

293

reasons — why I must wait until this afternoon,' said Gale.

'Well, you know your own business best,' said Fergusson, 'but you'll be cutting it rather fine, I'm thinking . . . '

'I am aware of that,' said Gale, 'but I can't help it . . . '

'I suppose it would be no good asking you to give me a hint . . . ?'

'No good at all . . . ' Gale shook his head.

Fergusson fumbled with his hat and gloves.

'What time this afternoon?' he asked abruptly.

'Half-past four.'

'I'll be here . . . ' He looked keenly at Gale. 'You're quite sure you *know*?'

'Yes — quite sure,' said Gale.

'If you're making a mistake there'll be no time to put it right . . . '

'I realize that,' said Simon, 'but I'm *not* making a mistake . . . '

'I hope not — for Mrs. Hallam's sake.' Fergusson got up. 'She's going through a dreadful ordeal, Mr. Gale — a terrible ordeal . . . '

'It will soon be ended now,' said Gale.

'Yes — but will it be ended in the right way,' said Fergusson, 'or with a noose — like that one you made in that piece of string? . . . '

'In the *right* way, Fergusson,' said Simon Gale. 'That noose is for quite a different person . . . '

II

The little clock on the mantelpiece began to strike four softly as Mrs Barrett came into the drawing-room.

'What time shall I bring in the tea, Miss Jill?' she asked.

'I'll ring, Mrs. Barrett,' said Jill. 'I think that will be best.'

Her cheeks were flushed from her walk with Martin, but she looked nervous and ill at ease. Simon Gale was showing signs of strain too. He prowled about the big room, pausing to touch ornaments and straighten pictures that were already straight.

'After you've brought in the tea, Mrs.

Barrett,' he said, 'I should like you to stay.'

'Stay?'

'Yes, you may as well learn the truth in company with the rest . . . '

'The truth, sir?'

'About the murder of Mr. Hallam,' he said.

She cleared her throat nervously.

'It wasn't — Mrs. Hallam?' she said.

'No,' he shook his head. 'It wasn't Mrs. Hallam . . . '

'Who was it?' asked the housekeeper. Her fingers rasped on the stiff material of her black dress.

'You'll hear later on,' said Gale. 'There's one thing I should like you to confirm. You stated in your evidence at the trial, that the front door was bolted in the morning, after you found Mr. Hallam's body. You're quite *sure* of that?'

'Yes, sir.'

'Were the windows all fastened?'

'Yes, sir. I always fasten them before going to bed. I fastened them that night as usual, and they were fastened in the morning. Except the little pantry window

— that's never fastened . . . '

'Thank you, that's all, Mrs. Barrett.'

She hesitated. Twice her lips parted as though she were on the point of asking something, but she didn't. In silence she went quietly out.

'Why did you go over all that again, Simon?' asked Jill, as the door closed.

'Just to make sure,' he answered.

She was silent for a little while, and then she said:

'Simon . . . '

'Yes?'

'I think I know what's in your mind . . . '

'Do you?' he said, non-committally.

'Yes, I think so . . . '

He refused the lead she offered.

'I wonder if you do?' he said. 'Well, you'll soon know . . . '

Martin came in.

'Nobody arrived yet?' he asked, going over to the fire.

'They're not due until half-past four,' said Gale.

'I'll be glad when it's all over,' said Martin. 'I don't know how you manage to keep so calm over it all, Simon.'

'I feel anything but calm, I assure you,' said Gale.

'I'm just a bundle of nerves,' confessed Jill.

'Well, neither of you look it,' said Martin. He took a cigarette out of his case with fingers that were not quite steady.

'Appearances can be very deceptive — you should remember that, Martin,' said his brother.

Martin on the point of replying, stiffened suddenly, as there came a loud double knock on the front door. They heard Mrs. Barrett cross the hall and open the door. A murmur of voices and then the housekeeper appeared at the door of the drawing-room.

'There's a gentleman to see Mr. Gale, Miss Jill,' she said.

'Ask him to come in,' said Gale, quickly.

'Who is it, Simon?' asked Jill.

'Someone I thought it might be useful to have here,' said Gale.

'This way, please, sir,' said Mrs. Barrett.

She ushered the newcomer into the room and Jill gave an exclamation of surprise as she saw who it was.

'Superintendent Shelford,' she cried.

'Good afternoon, Miss Hallam,' said Shelford.

'I'm glad you were able to come, Superintendent,' said Gale.

'I only hope it's not going to be a waste of time, sir,' said Shelford, in a slightly dubious tone.

'I don't think you'll find it will be,' said Gale.

'Well, I must admit your letter made me curious,' said Shelford. 'Mind you, I'm not saying that we've been wrong . . . '

'But there's a chance I may be right, eh?' Gale smiled.

Shelford shook his head.

'I'm not admitting that, sir,' he said.

'Well, it's very good of you to come,' said Gale. 'If I can convince you . . . '

'If you can convince me, Mr. Gale, that we made a mistake, I'll do everything I can to put it right,' said Shelford. 'You can count on that.'

'That's a bargain, Superintendent,' said Gale.

'Inspector Frost,' announced Mrs. Barrett.

'Hello, Frost,' greeted Shelford as the Inspector came in.

'Superintendent Shelford,' said Frost in surprise. 'Well, I never expected you'd be 'ere, an' that's a fact, sir . . . '

'Mr. Gale persuaded me against my better judgment,' said Shelford.

'Very glad I am to see you, sir,' said Frost, heartily.

'So am I,' said Simon Gale. 'You may get a surprise but I'm quite sure you won't be disappointed.'

III

It was barely half-past four when they began to arrive. Fergusson was the first, and he was quickly followed by Evershed. Almost on their heels came Vanessa and Mrs. Langdon-Humphreys. About them was an aura of nervous expectancy.

'Sit over here, Vanessa,' said Jill. 'We're

300

only waiting for Miss Ginch and then I'll ring for tea . . . '

'What's Mr. Gale going to do?' whispered Vanessa. 'I feel dreadfully nervous . . . '

'You know as much as I do,' answered Jill. 'You heard what he said this morning . . . '

'Did he really mean that?' said Vanessa. 'Is he going to tell us who — who killed Mr. Hallam?'

'That's why he's asked everybody here,' said Jill. She tried to conceal her excitement but it was evident in every movement she made, in the brightness of her eyes, and her flushed face.

'Does he *really* know?' asked Vanessa.

'If he does,' remarked Mrs. Langdon-Humphreys, 'I can see no reason for this unnecessarily melodramatic way of telling us . . . '

'There is nothing unnecessarily melo-dramatic about it, Mrs. Langdon-Humphreys,' said Gale. 'I'm sure, when you've heard what I have to say, you will agree that is the only *possible* way.'

'I should have imagined,' she answered,

by no means convinced, 'that the simplest way would have been to inform the police, and leave *them* to arrest the person concerned — presuming, of course, that you really *know* who it is . . .'

'You will shortly be in a position to judge whether I do or not,' retorted Gale.

'That seems fair enough,' said Evershed.

Mrs. Langdon-Humphreys eyed him coldly.

'I still consider, Doctor Evershed,' she said, 'that there was no need to adopt this procedure. It was most unpleasant for all of us. Any discoveries that Mr. Gale may have made should have been laid before Inspector Frost and Superintendent Shelford, who could have dealt with them in the proper manner . . .'

'I'm here entirely in an unofficial capacity, madam,' said Shelford.

'Oh, do stop making such a fuss,' interrupted Vanessa irritably.

'Really, Vanessa,' said Mrs. Langdon-Humphreys. 'That is not the way . . .'

'That's a most sensible remark, Miss

Lane,' interposed Major Fergusson. 'None of us was forced to come here — we came of our own free will to hear what Mr. Gale has to say . . . '

'Then I suggest,' said Mrs. Langdon-Humphreys, 'that Mr. Gale tells us without further delay . . . '

'We're not complete yet,' said Gale. 'As soon as Miss Ginch arrives . . . '

'Perhaps she isn't coming, Simon?' said Jill.

'Oh, yes, she'll come,' he declared confidently, and almost as he spoke Mrs. Barrett appeared to announce the late arrival.

'Oh, dear,' said Miss Ginch, tripping into the room in a fluster of contrition. 'I'm so sorry to be late, but I ran into the vicar, and he *would* discuss the arrangements for the Mothers' Outing. I thought I should *never* get away. So very awkward, you know . . . '

'Never mind, Miss Ginch,' said Jill. 'Come and sit over here, will you? You can bring tea now, Mrs. Barrett.'

'Yes, Miss Jill.' The housekeeper went out.

'Now that Miss Ginch *has* arrived,' said Mrs. Langdon-Humphreys, 'there can be no possible reason for keeping us waiting any longer, Mr. Gale.'

'No,' said Gale, 'there isn't. I should like Mrs. Barrett to be present but she will be back directly, so that's all right.' He moved to the centre of the fireplace. Standing with his back to the fire, he faced them. The room was charged with something akin to an electric current — the gathering of forces before a storm. 'When I first heard that Margaret Hallam had been convicted for the murder of her husband,' said Gale, after a slight pause, 'I knew there had been a mistake. I knew it as soon as I learned that he had been *poisoned*. It was *psychologically wrong* . . .'

'I'm afraid we had to judge by the evidence,' said Shelford, a little defensively.

'Yes,' Gale nodded. 'Fortunately I was not hampered by any such consideration. I'm not a detective. I know nothing about such things as cigar ash, fingerprints, alibis, and tangible clues of that kind.

Margaret Hallam is as incapable of poisoning anybody as she is of walking a tight-rope. I came here to find the real murderer, and I have. I know who killed John Hallam now . . . '

'Who?' demanded Evershed, curtly.

'The same person, who later killed Jonas Rigg, using practically an identical method, because Rigg had seen something on the night Hallam was killed that he *shouldn't* have seen . . . '

'Something — or *someone*, Simon?' asked Martin. He was very pale, and his hands gripped on the back of a chair behind which he was standing so that the bones of his knuckles stood out white.

'Someone,' said Gale.

'Mr. Upcott?' asked Vanessa. She, too, was white. Her fingers plucked at the cloth of her coat which she had not taken off. Jill looked at her and then at Martin, and her face was troubled.

'No, Vanessa,' answered Gale. 'It was *not* Upcott whom Rigg saw that night . . . '

'How do you know who it was he saw?' snapped Mrs. Langdon-Humphreys. 'The man's dead . . . '

'Yes, Mrs. Langdon-Humphreys — the man's dead,' said Gale. 'The person he saw took very good care that he should die before he could *say* what he saw . . . '

'Then how *can* you know?' she demanded.

'You'll see very soon,' he replied. 'There's only one person it *could* be . . . '

He stopped as the door opened and Mrs. Barrett came in. She pushed a dinner-wagon, laden with tea things, across the carpet to Jill's chair.

'Shut the door, Frost, will you?' said Gale. 'Mrs. Barrett is staying to hear the rest of what I have to say . . . '

The Inspector nodded and went over and closed the door.

'Perhaps,' said Gale, 'it would be as well if you locked it, Inspector.'

'Yes, sir,' said Frost. He turned the key, took it out of the lock, and slipped it into his pocket.

A queer whimpering sound came from Miss Ginch.

'I don't like it,' she said. 'I'm frightened! I wish to leave, Mr. Gale . . . '

'I'm afraid you'll have to stay until I've finished, Miss Ginch,' he said.

'I don't want to,' she cried, getting up quickly. 'I should much prefer to go home . . . '

'Sit down, Miss Ginch,' said Jill, soothingly. 'I'll give you a cup of tea . . . ' She began to put milk in the cups. She spoke calmly enough, but her hands were shaking.

'I don't want any tea,' said Miss Ginch, sharply. 'You've no right to keep me here . . . '

'Please be quiet, Miss Ginch,' said Gale.

'I won't . . . I'm not going to stay here . . . '

'Doctor Evershed,' said Jill, 'would you mind passing this to Miss Ginch?'

'Certainly,' he replied, taking the cup and saucer from her. 'Here you are, Miss Ginch . . . '

'I don't . . . ' she began.

'Please sit down,' said Simon Gale.

She started to make a further protest, thought better of it, and sat down again in her chair. Evershed put the cup and saucer into her hand.

'Drink that,' he said. 'You'll feel better . . . '

'I can understand Miss Ginch's nervousness,' said Gale. 'It is not pleasant to be locked in with a murderer . . . '

'You mean . . . ' It was a whisper from Mrs Langdon-Humphreys.

'Oh, yes,' said Gale, 'the person who poisoned Hallam and Rigg is here . . . '

Vanessa uttered a little sighing moan — as though she had been about to speak and caught her breath.

'Nearly all of you had a motive,' Gale went on. 'Hallam was a mental sadist. He liked to find out things about people — things they were afraid, or ashamed, of becoming public. He wasn't an ordinary blackmailer — he didn't want money. He wanted the pleasure of torturing his victims with the threat of exposure. He knew something about most of you, and it must have been a great relief when he died . . . '

'Can you pass this cup of tea to Simon, Vanessa?' whispered Jill.

'Eh?' said Vanessa with a start. 'Oh, yes . . . '

'But that wasn't a motive for his murder,' Gale continued. 'It was something much simpler than that . . . ' He paused, and Vanessa held out the cup of tea.

'Thank you,' he said, taking it, and then, seeing that she was without one, he added: 'Oh, look here, you have this, Vanessa . . . '

'No, no,' she answered quickly. 'It's all right . . . '

'Vanessa can have this one, Simon,' said Jill.

'No, really,' said Vanessa, 'you have it . . . '

'Will you drink this tea, Vanessa?' he said quietly, holding it out towards her.

'Well, I won't . . . I'm not in a hurry,' she stammered.

'Take it,' he said.

'Oh, well — if you insist . . . ' She took it from him reluctantly.

'Why are you making such a fuss, Simon?' said Jill. 'There's . . . '

'Don't touch that tea, Vanessa!' cried

Gale, as she was raising the cup to her lips. 'I've changed my mind . . . '

He almost snatched the cup and saucer from her hand.

'Jill shall drink it,' he said.

'I'll do nothing of the kind,' said Jill. 'What's the matter with you, Simon?'

'Drink this tea, Jill,' he ordered, thrusting the cup and saucer at her.

'I won't,' she answered.

'Why?' he snapped.

'Because it's ridiculous,' she retorted. 'First you want Vanessa to have it and when she won't . . . '.

'She *would*,' he said. 'She was going to — if I hadn't stopped her . . . '

'Well, *I* won't,' declared Jill, definitely. 'I think you've gone mad, Simon . . . '

'Frost,' said Gale, curtly. 'Search the pockets of Miss Lane's coat . . . '

'I object,' exclaimed Mrs. Langdon-Humphreys, angrily. 'How dare you . . . '

'I don't mind,' said Vanessa, putting her hands in her pockets. 'There's nothing . . . ' She stopped suddenly. Her face changed as she pulled out a little screw of tissue paper. 'Oh,' she said, starting at it, 'how did that get in my pocket . . . ?'

'Give it to me, Vanessa,' said Gale.

'What is it?' asked Shelford.

Gale unscrewed the paper and shook two little white pellets into the palm of his hand.

'I don't know how they got into my pocket,' said Vanessa, staring at them. 'I've — I've never seen them before . . . '

'You'd better take these, Doctor Evershed,' said Gale.

'That's what you put in the tea, Vanessa,' cried Jill, accusingly. 'I saw you — you dropped something in when you took it from me . . . '

'I didn't — I didn't drop anything in the tea . . . ' exclaimed Vanessa.

'Of course, you didn't,' began Mrs. Langdon-Humphreys.

'She did,' broke in Jill. 'I saw her, I tell you . . . That's why I wouldn't drink it . . . '

'It won't do, Jill,' said Gale, shaking his head. 'Vanessa was prepared to drink that tea. She wouldn't have done that, if she'd poisoned it. But that's why *you* wouldn't drink it. You were afraid that I really *did*

know who poisoned Hallam, weren't you?
. . . That I was coming out with the truth
— and you thought you could stop me by
poisoning the tea and throwing the blame
on Vanessa. *She* handed me the cup, and
you'd have sworn that you saw her drop
something in it. When the poison was
found in her pocket, which you had
slipped there earlier, the proof against her
would be complete . . . '

'*Jill*,' gasped Vanessa, in horror. 'Oh, no
. . . no . . . '

'It isn't true, Simon . . . ' began Jill.

'I suppose it was vanity that made you
think you'd get away with it?' continued
Gale, ignoring the interruption. 'You
never imagined that anyone would suspect *you*. You'd got away with it twice
when you killed Hallam and Rigg, and
you thought you could do it a third
time . . . ?'

16

I

'It's lies . . . all lies, Simon,' cried Jill, her face the colour of chalk, against which the make-up on her cheeks stood out garishly. 'You're just trying to save Margaret at any cost . . . '

'It's the truth,' said Simon Gale, 'and you know it's the truth. You were safe enough so long as no one began to suspect you. Once *that* happened, everything became clear . . . '

'I can't believe it,' muttered Vanessa, 'Jill . . . '

'Of course, you can't,' said Jill. 'It's not true, that's why. How *could* I have poisoned my father — I wasn't even *here* that night . . . '

'Oh, yes, you were,' broke in Gale. 'You went to London in the afternoon, but you came back later . . . you came back and waited outside the study window until

313

you saw Maggie bring your father the glass of hot whisky and milk, which you knew she did every night. As soon as she'd gone to bed you came in through the french window, made some plausible excuse to Hallam, and dropped the barbitone into the hot drink. You'd taken it from Maggie's drawer before you left — it was easy for *you* to get hold of the key, she had a habit of leaving her bag lying around . . . '

'I didn't . . . I tell you, I didn't!' cried Jill. 'Why should I want to kill my father . . . ?'

'You wanted to kill them *both* — that was the whole idea,' said Gale, 'but you thought you could safely leave Maggie's death to the hangman. *That* way left *you* free of all suspicion. As a further safeguard, once Maggie had been convicted, you pretended that you were convinced of her innocence. You did everything you could to try and help her, believing that the evidence was *so* strong against her that nothing you could do would have any effect. But it *looked* good, didn't it? People thought it was so sweet and kind of you, and that was the impression you wanted to create. How could anyone imagine that the girl who was working *so* hard to try and save her stepmother had planned the whole thing . . . ?'

'You're mad, Simon,' cried Jill. 'Mad. Why should I do all this?'

'For the commonest motive in the world,' he answered. 'Money.'

'Money?' muttered Fergusson.

'Until Hallam married again,' Gale went on, still addressing Jill, 'his fortune would have come to *you* on his death. But once *Maggie* came on the scene it was a different matter. The greater part of his money would go to *her*. You weren't going to stand for *that*, and so you began to scheme how you could get it all. You hated Maggie from the first, didn't you? But you were clever enough to *pretend* that you liked her while you waited your opportunity . . . '

'It's lies . . . lies, I tell you . . . ' An ugly glitter had appeared in Jill's eyes and her mouth twisted almost in a snarl. The dainty prettiness was there still but it had been *smeared* . . .

'That opportunity came,' Simon Gale went on relentlessly, 'when Hallam threatened to alter his will. Mrs. Barrett overheard him, and you knew that she would bear witness to the fact. It supplied Maggie with a strong motive, which is what you'd been waiting for. You decided to put the plan, which you'd had in your mind for so long, into practice at once — that same night. Your alibi was easy enough to fake. Martin went to that hotel where you stayed . . . '

'*Martin* . . . ' breathed Jill.

'Yes, that's what he went to London for,' said Gale. 'You were there for dinner, but nobody saw you *after*. You were supposed to have gone to bed early, but there's a service staircase close to the room you occupied — it's easy to come and go without being seen, and you were back in your room and in bed before they brought you your tea in the morning. It was all so simple. The evidence against Maggie was so strong that the police didn't burrow very deeply into *your* alibi. If they had they'd have found how weak it was. But you *were* seen that night — you were seen by Jonas Rigg. He didn't think there was anything strange about it — *until* he learned that you were supposed to have been in London, and he didn't learn *that* until he came out of prison a few days ago . . . '

'No . . . *no*, Simon . . . '

He ignored her outburst.

'Rigg had to die — a word from him would have blown your clever scheme sky high. You adopted the same method you'd used before, only *this* time you tried to throw suspicion on Vanessa. You knew that note would bring her to the caravan *after* Rigg was dead, and we were all there. You knew she wouldn't dare produce it because of what it contained. That was when I first began to see *you* as the murderer, Jill. *You* were the only person, except Martin and myself, who knew that Rigg was going to tell us something that night. You also knew, before you'd had a chance of seeing, *where the lamp was kept*. Remember?'

'It doesn't prove anything,' she cried. 'Nothing . . . nothing . . . '

'It's not all,' said Gale. 'When we first saw Rigg in the Hand and Flower and the landlord told him to get out, do you remember what he said?'

'No . . . no . . . ' She was breathing fast as though she had been running, 'he didn't say anything . . . '

'He said: *'Afraid of upsetting the gentry? I don't go round poisoning people like some I could name . . . ''*

'Well, supposing he did?' she demanded.

'It was a warning, Jill,' said Gale. 'He was trying to tell somebody that he *knew*, and there was nobody else in the pub except you and I, and Martin. *He couldn't have meant it for us.*'

'It's absurd . . . ridiculous . . . ' she exclaimed.

'When we went to Rigg's caravan later that Sunday, Jill, you answered that veiled threat of his,' said Gale. 'You said: *'Don't make a mistake, Rigg. It's very important. I'll see that you're well paid.'* You were telling him, as plainly as you could, to keep his mouth shut . . . It all fits in, Jill . . . '

'You're *making* it fit,' cried Jill. 'You're

twisting everything . . . '

'You were so *sure*, weren't you? You felt *safe*, and then, when I told you I *knew*, you began to wonder. Could I really have stumbled on the truth?' Gale leaned forward and Jill involuntarily shrank back. 'You were suddenly afraid then. Something had to be done, just in case, and so you poisoned that tea. *That* would destroy the only danger, and get Vanessa out of the way, too — the same trick of killing two birds with one stone. You'd fallen in love with Martin, and you wanted a clear field . . . '

'Oh, no,' whispered Vanessa, 'no . . . '

'That's why you were to be the victim, Vanessa,' said Gale. 'Well, the plan failed. The third time *wasn't lucky*, because I was *expecting* you to do just what you *did* do, Jill. I knew that if I frightened you enough, you'd do something to ensure your safety. I told you at the beginning that we'd catch the murderer because it would be impossible to leave well alone. And if you were going to do anything, you *had* to do it this afternoon — before I had a chance of talking. I made it as easy as I could for you — and you fell into the trap . . . '

Jill Hallam's face contorted. There was not even the remnants of the dainty prettiness, now . . .

'You devil, Simon,' she ground out from between her teeth, 'you clever devil . . . '

'Your father had a queer kink, and it's been passed on to you,' Gale was deliberately taunting. 'Only it took a different turn with you. Hell's bells, how you've fooled everybody. But the mask has slipped *now*. We can see right through to the *meanness* behind, and the secretive, cowardly, *slyness* that breeds the poisoner . . . '

'Stop it!' She screamed suddenly losing the last of her control. 'Stop it, stop it, stop it . . . ' She made a spring at Gale, her fingers clawing . . .

'Look out, sir,' warned Frost, but Shelford already had her by the wrists.

'I've got her,' he said.

'Let go of me . . . let me go . . . ' She fought hard, biting and scratching.

'Don't you wish I'd drunk that tea, Jill?' said Gale.

'Yes, yes.' She hardly knew what she was saying in the flood of fury that welled over her. 'I wish I hadn't waited so long . . . but I never thought you'd find out . . . '

'Not so clever as you imagined,' said Gale, contemptuously. 'People like you never are. It's the kink that makes them think they are . . . '

'I was clever . . . I *was* clever,' she shrieked at him, struggling in Shelford's grip. 'It would have been all right if it hadn't been for you . . . I always hated Margaret . . . ever since she came here . . . and I hated my father, too . . . I wanted life and fun — there was neither here, and I couldn't get away . . . only if I had money . . . '

'Oh . . . ' The voice of Mrs. Barrett, broken and tearful, sounded through her raving. 'Miss Jill . . . Oh, Miss Jill . . . '

'*She* knows,' Jill swung round towards the housekeeper. 'She knows what it was like — living here . . . '

'I think that's enough, Superintendent,'

said Gale to Shelford.

'Yes, sir, I think so, too,' he agreed.

'You can't touch me,' screamed Jill, hysterically . . . 'It's Margaret you want . . . Margaret . . . '

'Oh, dear,' said Miss Ginch, 'she's mad . . . quite mad . . . '

'I'm not . . . I'm not mad,' a little bubbling foam appeared on the drawn back lips. 'I hate Margaret . . . I want her to hang . . . Do you hear? . . . I want her to hang . . . '

'Be careful,' said Doctor Evershed warningly.

'You'd better take her away, Frost,' said Gale.

'No . . . ' She cried, sobbing and laughing in a dreadful animal-like mixture of sounds. 'I won't go . . . I won't . . . leave me alone . . . '

'Now come along, miss,' said Frost, soothingly. 'It's no good making a fuss . . . '

'I'd better go with you, I think,' said Evershed.

'If you would, doctor,' said Frost, gratefully. 'Now, come along . . . '

With the help of Shelford he managed to get the struggling, screaming girl to the door. They could hear her screams die away . . .

'Oh,' Vanessa began to cry softly. 'It's horrible, horrible . . . '

'Don't,' said Martin, putting his arm around her, 'don't darling . . . '

'Oh, Martin,' she gulped and buried her head on his shoulder.

Simon Gale wiped his face with his handkerchief. He looked strained and shaken.

'I'm sorry,' he said, 'but I had to push her over the edge . . . There wasn't any real evidence, you know . . . '

'I think,' said Mrs. Langdon-Humphreys indignantly, 'that you might have spared us . . . '

'There was no other way,' he said.

'You've saved Mrs. Hallam,' said Fergusson. 'That's the main thing . . . '

'That rests with the Home Secretary,' said Gale.

'I don't think there'll be any difficulty there, sir?' Superintendent Shelford came back in time to hear what he said. 'Not when he hears what I have to tell him . . . '

Mrs. Barrett, who had been sobbing quietly, raised a tear-stained face.

'Poor Miss Jill,' she said, 'poor, poor, Miss Jill . . . she's the image of her mother — but she's got her father's nature, that's the trouble — her father's nature . . . '

II

It was a perfect spring afternoon. The sun flooded Easton Knoll and the distant trees looked like fine green gauze thrown over bare brown branches. The sun poured in through the open windows of the drawing-room making the whole room brighter and more cheerful.

Simon Gale puffing contentedly at his pipe looked across at Margaret Hallam sitting in a big chair, idly staring about the room.

'Nice to be home again, Maggie?' he said.

She smiled, a warm, happy smile.

'Yes . . . oh, yes, Simon,' she said. 'I love this house, although I haven't been very happy here . . . '

'That's all over,' he said quickly. 'You've got to forget all that . . . '

She shook her head.

'I shall never forget — however long I live . . . '

'Nonsense, of course you will,' he said impatiently. 'It's wonderful how quickly one can forget unpleasant things . . . much quicker than pleasant things. I suppose it's because one wants to . . . '

'I shall never forget one thing,' she said seriously, 'that I owe you my life.'

'It was a near thing, Maggie,' he declared. 'I was in a sweat of fear that afternoon that something would go wrong. If Jill hadn't reacted as I hoped she would, we'd have been sunk . . . '

'What first made you suspect her, Simon?' she asked.

'Well, to be absolutely accurate,' he replied, 'you did . . . '

'*Me?*' she said in astonishment.

'Yes — it was when I came up to see you that day,' said Gale. 'You were talking about Vanessa. You said: 'She's pretending all the time. She wants you to think she's one kind of person, while, in reality, she's something quite different . . . ''

'I remember. You started talking about a box of conjuring tricks you had when you were a boy.' She laughed, it was a low, pleasant sound. 'I couldn't make out what you meant . . . '

'The art of misdirection,' said Gale. 'It suddenly struck me, then, that if we applied what you'd said about *Vanessa* to *Jill*, it led to an entirely fresh view-point. Everything began to drop neatly into place. Motive, opportunity, means — Jill had all of them. And she was the right *type*. I couldn't understand why I hadn't seen it before. It was so obvious . . . '

'I never thought of Jill for a moment,' said Margaret.

'No, that's because she played her part so cleverly,' he answered. 'She put us off by her pretended anxiety to try and save you. Everybody thought it was because she was fond of you . . . '

'I always thought she quite liked me . . . '

'If she hadn't adopted *that* camouflage, she'd probably have been my first suspect,' said Simon. 'The motive stood out like an iceberg in the Sahara. With you and Hallam out of the way, she got all the money. When once I began to suspect her, the more I thought about it, the more certain I was that I was right. It accounted for Rigg's behaviour and everything. But I had no proof, not a scrap that would have been any good. I *had* to make her give herself away. If she'd just done *nothing*, I couldn't have proved a thing against her. But I was sure she would *have* to do something. She was getting nervy with the strain, and she was afraid. It was almost impossible that she would have the courage to leave well alone. She didn't know how *much* I knew, and I gambled on her trying to stop me talking. It was a certainty that if she *did*, she'd use poison, and that she'd try and throw the blame on Vanessa. She'd tried to do that once, when she killed Rigg, and I was pretty sure she'd do it again. She hated Vanessa because of Martin . . . '

'What was in the tea — barbitone?' asked Margaret.

'No — cyanide. Barbitone would have taken too long in this instance. It had to be something swift ... a few seconds ...'

'She took a tremendous risk — with everybody there ...'

'No — that was her safeguard. She'd planted those tablets of cyanide in Vanessa's pocket, and she made *Vanessa* pass me the tea. If the plan had worked, and I'd died, she'd have accused Vanessa, and I doubt very much if anybody would have suspected Jill. It wasn't such a risk as letting me tell what I *might* know ...'

'Will you see Inspector Frost, sir?' said Mrs. Barrett, appearing in the doorway.

'Yes, show him in,' said Gale.

'Poor Mrs. Barrett,' said Margaret, when the housekeeper had gone. 'She looks terribly ill ...'

'She was very fond of Jill,' answered Gale. 'It was rather a shock for her, poor soul ...'

'Perhaps it would do her good if she went away for a holiday,' said Margaret.

Inspector Frost was ushered in.

'How do you do, Mrs. Hallam,' he said.
'Good afternoon, sir.'

'Sit down, Inspector,' said Margaret. 'I have a great deal to thank you for . . . '

'It's Mr. Gale you've got to thank, ma'am,' said Frost, 'an' that's a fact.'

'But you helped enormously . . . '

'Yes, he did,' said Gale. 'How's Miss Hallam, now, Frost?'

The Inspector shook his head.

'Gone *right* over the edge, sir,' he said. 'Doctor Evershed's with her. We had to put a trained nurse to look after her all night. It was the shock. They can't face finding out they're not as clever as they thought they were, you know . . . '

Margaret's face clouded.

'I can't help feeling sorry . . . ' she said, softly.

'You needn't,' said Gale. 'It's going to save her a lot of suffering . . . '

'More than she deserves, if you ask me, sir,' said Frost. 'You don't know where you are with a poisoner. If she'd got away with it, she'd have gone on doing it — they always do . . . '

'Yes, you're quite right,' said Gale.

'I came to tell you that Upcott's dead,' went on Frost. "'E died early this morning . . . '

'That's also going to save a great deal of trouble, Inspector,' said Simon.

'That's a fact,' said Frost. 'We found Mrs. Upcott's body — he'd buried it under the rockery in the garden — but it would have been difficult to prove whether 'e killed 'er, or whether it was an accident as 'e said . . . '

'I think he was speaking the truth there,' said Gale.

'Well,' said Frost, with a sigh, 'it doesn't really matter, I s'pose. You know it's a wonder 'e didn't run into Miss 'Allam that night . . . '

'Yes, she must have been there when he came,' said Gale.

'What makes you think that, sir?'

'Because *she* must have bolted the front door, after he'd left,' explained Simon. 'She probably heard him coming and hid until he'd gone . . . '

'That must 'ave been a nasty moment for 'er . . . ' grunted the Inspector. "'Old

330

on, though — 'ow did she get out of the 'ouse — everything was fastened . . . ?'

'Except the pantry window,' said Gale. 'It's too small for anyone else, but Jill could have squeezed through easily. I think that was when Rigg saw her . . . '

There was the sound of voices in the hall and Martin and Vanessa came in.

'Come on, Vanessa,' cried Martin, 'let's tell them the news . . . '

'Congratulations!' said Gale.

'But he hasn't told you what it is . . . ' said Vanessa.

'Hell's bells, it's been obvious for days,' retorted Simon.

'I only asked her an hour ago,' said Martin.

'It was a foregone conclusion that you would sooner or later,' said his brother, 'and equally evident what her answer would be . . . '

'I wish *I'd* been so certain,' declared Martin fervently. 'I wouldn't have been so nervous . . . '

'*I* didn't notice anything *nervous* about you, Martin,' said Vanessa.

'I don't suppose he was, really,' said

Margaret, laughing. 'I can't imagine a *Gale* being nervous. I hope you'll be very happy . . . '

'Thank you, Margaret,' said Vanessa. She hesitated for a moment and then she said, in a rush: 'I'm so very, very glad everything is — is all right . . . '

'It's rather like coming out of a nightmare,' said Margaret. 'I'm going to have a long, long rest . . . '

'I'm afraid I must be off,' interrupted Inspector Frost. 'There's still a lot to do, an' that's a fact . . . Goodbye, Mrs. 'Allam . . . '

'Goodbye, Inspector,' said Margaret. 'I shall always be grateful for what you did . . . '

'I ought to 'ave done it earlier, ma'am, an' saved you a lot of unhappiness . . . Goodbye, Mr. Gale . . . ' Simon escorted him to the door.

'Nice chap, Frost,' he said when he came back. 'What does Mrs. Langdon-Humphreys say about you two?'

'She doesn't know yet,' said Vanessa.

'We're going to break it to her, now,' said Martin.

'I don't think she'll mind,' said Vanessa, 'she was talking last night about giving up the house and taking a flat in London.'

'I think in the circumstances, it would be a good thing,' said Simon.

'There's one thing I don't understand, Simon,' said Martin, suddenly. 'If Hallam was going to alter his will there was no need for Jill to — to . . . '

'I don't think he was,' said Gale. 'I think that telephone call to old Mayhew was Jill's idea . . . '

'How do you mean, Simon?' asked Margaret.

'It made the evidence stronger against you, Maggie,' he answered. 'She could easily have found some excuse for getting her father to ask Mayhew down — probably something to do with that unpleasant little hobby of his . . . '

'Do you think she *knew* about that?' said Margaret.

'She must have done . . . '

'Why?' asked Vanessa.

'She couldn't have sent that note to you unless she knew, could she?' he said. 'And

333

she could only have known through Hallam . . . '

'Yes, I see . . . '

'Anyway, if Hallam had intended to alter his will in a fit of temper, there was no saying when he might decide to alter it back again,' said Gale.

Margaret got up quickly.

'Don't let's talk about it any more . . . '

'We must be going,' said Martin. 'I promised to take Vanessa back for tea . . . '

'Have you decided when you're getting married?' said Margaret.

'Not yet,' said Martin, 'but it will be as soon as possible . . . '

'You'll stay here for a week or two, won't you,' she said, 'you and Simon?'

'Of course,' said Simon Gale. 'I'm going to do what I've always wanted to do, Maggie — paint you . . . '

'Miss Ginch says that . . . that . . . ' Vanessa stopped and reddened.

'What's that scandal-mongering old busybody spreading around now?' demanded Gale.

'Well . . . ' Vanessa was a little

334

embarrassed. 'She says she's quite sure it won't be long before you and Margaret are — ' She stopped and Margaret looked at Simon and laughed.

'There's nothing like that between Simon and me,' she declared.

'Hell's bells!' cried Gale, 'I wouldn't marry a woman with Maggie's temper . . . '

'And I certainly don't want to marry you, Simon,' she said. 'I couldn't stand a husband who will insist on calling me Maggie . . . '

He grinned.

'Always got you in a temper, didn't it?' he said.

'Yes, it did,' she answered. 'It still does . . . '

'Good!' he cried. 'I hope I can get you into *such* a temper that it will last long enough to paint. It would be a wonderful picture, Maggie, a wonderful picture . . . '

THE MAN IN THE DARK

Donald Stuart

In Burma, the British manager of the ruby mines of Mogok has been away, attempting to track down a leopard that had been attacking livestock. He returns to discover his stand-in at the office lying dead on the floor, the safe door open and its contents stolen. Fifty of the mine's finest rubies had been awaiting shipment to the company's London office. Those jewels, seemingly endowed with evil powers, are destined to cause numerous men to meet their deaths . . .